DATE DUE

THE TAMING OF ANNABELLE

THE TAMING OF ANNABELLE

MARION CHESNEY

St. Martin's Press
New York

Library of Congress Cataloging in Publication Data

Chesney, Marion.
   The taming of Annabelle.

   I. Title.
PR6053.H4535T3   1984   823'.914   83-21145
ISBN 0-312-78489-9

First published in Great Britain in 1983 by Macdonald & Co.
(Publishers) Ltd.

First U.S. Edition

10 9 8 7 6 5 4 3 2 1

The Maunder's Praise of his
strowling Mort

Doxy, oh! thy glaziers shine
As glimmar; by the Salomon!
No gentry mort has prats like thine,
No cove e'er wap'd with such a one.

White thy fambles, red thy gan,
And thy quarrons dainty is;
Couch a hogshead with me then,
In the darkmans clip and kiss ...

                              Anon

* W.H. Auden's *Oxford Book of Light Verse*, Oxford University Press

CHAPTER ONE

The only sign that the Armitage family was rising out of the mire of debt into which they had sunk the year before was the addition of two splendid hunters to the Reverend Charles Armitage's stable and several highly bred hounds to his pack.

Rigorous economy was still practised in the vicarage. Meals were of the cheapest cuts of meat, and clothes were still darned and altered and handed down.

The vicar of St Charles and St Jude in the village of Hopeworth had eight children, six girls and twin boys. His eldest daughter Minerva, now twenty years of age, had only a month before announced her engagement to Lord Sylvester Comfrey, the Duke of Allsbury's youngest son. The Armitage brood had somehow hoped this forthcoming noble alliance would immediately pour gold into the coffers of the vicarage. But although Lord Sylvester and his friend Peter, Marquess of Brabington, had generously lent the vicar money, and Lord Sylvester had lent him the use of his steward so that the tenant farms should flourish under professional guidance, no immediate signs of any affluence were to be felt.

The vicar had explained that the money must be paid back as soon as possible, not only to his daughter's fiancé and to the Marquess, but also to Lady Godolphin for the expense that lady had incurred in bringing Minerva out.

The twins, Peregrine and James, aged ten, admittedly had their future education at Eton secured, but for the girls and Mrs Armitage life went on much as it had done before Minerva's engagement.

Christmas passed quietly. Minerva was to be married in March and her younger sisters were already tearfully pleading for new gowns to be made for the wedding.

Apart from Minerva, there was Annabelle, seventeen,

7

Deirdre, fifteen, Daphne, fourteen, Diana, thirteen, and Frederica, aged twelve.

Annabelle, the next in line, suffered from a nagging feeling of discontent which had nothing to do with her family's straitened circumstances.

She had fallen in love at first sight with her sister Minerva's fiancé, Lord Sylvester Comfrey.

The admiration of his lordship's friend, the Marquess of Brabington, had been noticed by Annabelle and quickly discounted as unimportant.

At first, it had been the Marquess of Brabington who had occupied her dreams. He had descended on the vicarage to explain that he and Lord Sylvester Comfrey had decided to help the impoverished family out of their predicament by restoring the vicar's land to good heart. The Marquess had given the vicar a generous loan and had then proceeded to win the hearts of the Armitage family in general and Annabelle in particular. He had walked with her about the village and the neighbouring countryside, implying by every look and gesture a closer, warmer relationship to follow. He had reluctantly left, telling Annabelle he must rejoin his regiment, but that he hoped to return as soon as possible.

But then Lord Sylvester had followed Minerva from London, Minerva who had run away – inexplicably, from all those sophisticated delights – and had proposed marriage. One look at Lord Sylvester, and the fond memory of the Marquess of Brabington shrivelled and died in Annabelle's pretty head.

Her every waking minute seemed filled with thoughts of Lord Sylvester. She had not seen him since his monumental visit when the engagement was announced. Minerva and Mrs Armitage had departed for a month's visit to Lord Sylvester's parents' home. But absence was turning love into an obsession. Annabelle felt that Lord Sylvester was making a dreadful mistake. Minerva would not make him a suitable wife.

Minerva was strict and prosy. How she had managed to capture a handsome and dashing rake like Comfrey was

8

beyond any of Annabelle's wildest imaginings. Admittedly, Minerva was very beautiful with her black hair and wide, clear, grey eyes. But she, Annabelle, knew that her own looks were startling. Fashion might decree that blondes were 'unfortunate' but Annabelle Armitage had learnt at an early age that the combination of golden hair, blue eyes, a trim figure and neat ankles had a delightful effect on any gentleman in the county of Berham.

Hadn't she nearly been engaged herself and well before Minerva? But Guy Wentwater had turned out to be a slave trader and so the engagement had never come to pass. And then just as her feelings towards him were becoming warm again, he had mysteriously disappeared, and even his aunt, Lady Wentwater, swore she had not heard a word from him.

Mrs Armitage, who loved to believe herself ill with all kinds of humours and strange infections, had left Minerva to be head of the household. With Minerva and her mother gone, Annabelle found she once more had to take over the tiresome duties of the household and the parish.

And the more she did, the more she became convinced that Minerva's natural role was that of spinster. Minerva had shown all signs of contentment with the dull routine of village life. Annabelle had always kicked and railed against it. Therefore, it followed – so ran Annabelle's busy thoughts – that should Lord Sylvester decide he would be better suited with the younger sister then it would not be doing Minerva any great disservice.

That prim lady would suffer a little hurt, a little grief, but that was all. Minerva could surely never suffer from the strong passionate feelings which were churning around in her own bosom.

But how could she even begin to plan to take Lord Sylvester's affections away from Minerva, if Lord Sylvester himself were never present to be charmed?

Although the vicarage boasted a cook housekeeper, a housemaid, an odd man, and a coachman, Annabelle was expected to help with the household chores. As these

9

thoughts ran through her head, she was engaged in removing grease spots from the plush upholstery of the dining chairs, a messy business which involved rubbing the stains gently with hot bread rolls.

Minerva and her mother were not expected home until the afternoon and Annabelle planned to put on her best dress just in case Lord Sylvester accompanied them.

She did not, therefore, even pause from her task at the sound of carriage wheels on the weedy gravel of the short drive outside, assuming her father had returned from his parish rounds.

Then she dropped the last roll in consternation as her mother's plaintive voice sounded outside, saying, 'Is there *no one* to welcome me?'

Annabelle ran to the window and looked out. If Lord Sylvester had arrived then she would escape to her room and prettify herself as fast as she could.

But there was only the small person of Mrs Armitage who was languidly directing a brace of magnificent footmen to be careful with the baggage.

Lord Sylvester's coach had arrived, but without either his lordship or Minerva.

Annabelle ran out and hugged her mother and planted a kiss on that lady's withered cheek.

'Mama! Where is Minerva? Why are you come alone?'

'I feel monstrous travel sick,' said Mrs Armitage faintly, disengaging herself from her daughter's embrace. 'Do not fuss so, child. I must lie down. I can feel one of my Spasms coming on.'

But Annabelle, unlike Minerva, was not to be intimidated by her mother's famous Spasms. 'You *cannot* disappear to your room, Mama, without first giving me intelligence of your visit. How do they live? Are they very grand?'

'Oh, very well,' sighed Mrs Armitage, capitulating. 'But let me indoors to remove my bonnet and tell Mrs Hammer to fetch me a dish of tea.' Mrs Hammer was the cook housekeeper.

Annabelle fled to the kitchen and was soon back to join

10

her mother who was seated by the fire in the parlour.

'It's so *good* to be home,' said Mrs Armitage. 'The Duke and Duchess of Allsbury live in *such* a grand manner. And so many guests, coming and going! And the clothes, my dear. The fashions! I felt quite the country dowd, although Minerva lent me some items from her wardrobe. It is as well that Lady Godolphin was so generous. Not that her grace is too high in the instep. She gave me a good recipe for Shrewsbury cake which surpasses ours. And she ...'

'But what of *Minerva*?' interrupted Annabelle impatiently.

'Oh, Minerva seems quite accustomed to the grand life. I declare, you would think she had been bred to it. Not that Lady Godolphin could have taught her much in the way of decorum for that lady arrived when we were staying there and I was never more shocked. She dresses like laced mutton and mixes up all her words. Kept referring to dear Lord Sylvester as Minerva's "fancy". I only realized after a time, she meant fiancé. The Duchess is to furnish the bride's gown, which is a blessing. Thousands of guineas it must have cost. Real Brussels lace over white satin and a vastly fetching cottage bonnet of Brussels lace with two feathers and ...'

'Mama!' said Annabelle slowly and carefully. '*Where* is Minerva and why has she not returned?'

'Because of *you*, my dear,' exclaimed Mrs Armitage.

Annabelle suddenly blushed. Had Minerva discovered, somehow, her secret passion for Lord Sylvester?

In a daze, she heard her mother going on, 'Minerva felt it would be a good opportunity for you to go on a visit to meet some suitable gentleman and become accustomed to the ways of the ton since you are too young to make your come-out ...'

'I am seventeen!' protested Annabelle, though her heart had begun to beat erratically. She would see *him* again.

'To meet some young gentleman,' pursued Mrs Armitage. 'The Duke's servants are putting up at the inn and you are to travel tomorrow ...'

'Tomorrow! I have nothing to wear.'

'Well, as to that. Lady Godolphin gave Minerva a most extensive wardrobe and you are of a size. Such a disgraceful old lady. She is only a distant relation of mine, some sort of cousin who isn't far enough removed. I must say there has always been bad blood in that family. Now, I am fatigued with the journey and there are your things to be packed. Tell Betty' – Betty was the housemaid – 'she is to help you pack and prepare to travel with you, since you must have a maid. And put on your bonnet and go to Mr Macdonald's shop and choose some silk ribbons to trim your blue velvet gown which will just be the thing for travelling in this weather.'

Annabelle tried to find out more about the Duke's residence, and who was staying there at present and who were these young men she was to meet, but Mrs Armitage only closed her eyes and languidly complained of the headache and so Annabelle had to content herself with saving all her questions for the evening.

The day was steel grey and cold as she walked towards the village of Hopeworth. A faint powdering of snow dusted the thatch of the houses and lay on the frozen ruts in the road.

Annabelle's brain was in a whirl. For the first time, her supreme self confidence began to fail and she experienced a qualm of fright at the thought of meeting high society in the mass for the first time. What vails did one give the servants, for example? And did one give them money when one arrived or when one left?

But Minerva would know, she thought with a sigh of relief. And straight after that pleasant thought came one of pure irritation that her sister, her rival, should know to a nicety as to how to go on with members of the ton when she, Annabelle, did not.

The shop was fairly busy and Mr Macdonald's young men were pivoting themselves over the counter with amazing ease, their faces shining and their coat tails flying. Farmers and country people from the neighbourhood were standing around, sleeking down their hair, and glancing shyly about as they summoned up the courage to ask one of the smart young shop assistants to find them some notion to take back to their wives or daughters.

Annabelle was turning over various colours of silk ribbons in a box when two young exquisites entered the store.

'I know it's all very rustic and these yokels do stare so, George,' drawled one, 'but a chap can find amazing bargains in these backwaters.'

'If you say so, Cyril,' said his companion with a little titter.

Annabelle studied them covertly. Both were slap up to the nines in blue swallowtail coats and Marseilles waistcoats. They smelled strongly of musk. Their hair was teased and curled and pomaded. Although the one called George had brown hair, and his friend Cyril, black, they somehow looked remarkably alike. But one thing was evident to Annabelle, both were Pinks of the Ton.

She decided to listen to their conversation to see if she could pick up some crumbs of fashionable speech to use on her visit.

'How's Barry?' asked the one called George.

'Oh, still at College. Got enough money to pay chummage though. Got two chums to rough it sleeping on the stairs. I told him not to play in that low dive. That Greek ivory turner used a bale of bard cinque deuces on him so its all Dicky with poor Barry. He was in his altitudes at the time. Well, now he's in the nask. See here, fellow, let me see a bale of that sea green silk.'

'Sea green. Sea sick,' laughed George.

Both took out long quizzing glasses and squinted at the material.

'What you want it for?' demanded George.

'Coat ... to wear at Almack's next Season.'

'No, no, no, dear chap!' exclaimed Cyril, raising his white hands in horror. 'They'll think you're Henry Cope. Can't wear *green*. Definitely old hat, dear boy.'

George let out an almost feminine scream of laughter. 'Oh, let's be on our journey. I do not know why you must

13

stop in these dingy places.'

They drifted out, arm in arm, leaving a strong aroma of musk behind them.

'It's not my place to criticize my betters,' said a burly coachman roundly. 'But them back gammon players make me want to flash my hash. Oh, I *beg* your pardon, Miss. I forgot you was there. I hope you didn't understand what they were saying. Not for the ears of a lady.'

'I didn't hear a word,' lied Annabelle sweetly.

'That's a mercy,' said the coachman. 'It's all the fashion for them fribbles to talk coachee as they calls it, but there's few of us would use that sort of cant, 'specially when there's ladies around.'

He moved away to buy green tea at the opposite counter and Annabelle turned all the mysterious conversation she had heard over in her mind.

She had heard that it was fashionable to use coachman's slang and underworld cant. Now Minerva would *never* use a cant word but would not she, Annabelle, appear to advantage if she mastered the art? The men had not been saying anything very bad, after all. They had been talking about some friend at college. And then they had said green was 'old hat'. Well, that obviously meant something that was no longer fashionable.

It is to be understood that Annabelle was suffering from a kind of mini-madness. She no longer paused to think much about the fact that plotting to take Lord Sylvester away from her sister was wrong. Annabelle had always rather despised Minerva, much as she loved her. Minerva always seemed to be moralizing about something, and although much of the old priggish, martyred Minerva had disappeared since her engagement, she had not been home much, and, in any case, Annabelle, blinded by jealousy, had noticed no change. The lovelight shining in Minerva's eyes seemed to her younger sister very much the manifestation of Minerva's former do-goody fervor.

She did not think for one moment that Minerva was passionately in love with Lord Sylvester. Minerva had been sent to London to catch a rich husband so that the

14

failing Armitage fortunes might be saved. Had not papa told her she must be a martyr? And so Minerva had martyred herself. Now, should Lord Sylvester prefer the fair Annabelle, then there would be no harm done. The Comfrey money would be kept in the family.

These cheerful thoughts occupied Annabelle's mind after she had purchased the ribbons and was walking home towards the vicarage. At dinner that evening Mrs Armitage was irritatingly vague about the Duke's residence. Lord Sylvester had, of course, his own estate. The Allsbury mansion was called Haeter Abbey, Haeter being one of the family names. Yes, it was large. Yes, there were a lot of servants. But although Annabelle's four younger sisters, just back from school in nearby Hopeminster also plied their mother with questions, none of them could gain a clear picture of Haeter Abbey. The twins were in London, cramming for Eton at a preparatory school.

Then Annabelle noticed that fifteen-year-old Deirdre was wearing one of her best dresses and had put her red hair up.

'How dare you!' snapped Annabelle. 'Sitting there like a guy. Do talk to her, mama. That is one of my gowns which Betty should have packed.'

'It is very becoming with her unfortunate colour of hair,' said Mrs Armitage. 'Minerva will have many gowns for you, Annabelle. You should not grudge your little sister one.'

'Deirdre is thoroughly spoiled,' sniffed Annabelle, who like most of the human race was quick to criticize her own faults in others. 'Go upstairs this instant, miss, and take it off.'

'If you wish,' whispered Deirdre, 'but I shall tell papa that you are in love with Lord Sylvester.'

'Hey, what's that?' demanded the vicar from the head of the table.

Annabelle felt her cheeks burning. 'I was just telling Deirdre that she may keep my gown,' she said.

'Oh, hey! Women's stuff,' said the vicar. 'Which

15

reminds me, I'll have a word with you after dinner, Bella.'

Annabelle eyed her father nervously. He was a thickset man with a round, ruddy face and small, twinkling shoe-button eyes. Although he appeared to give all his thoughts to his horses and his pack, he sometimes had an uncanny knack of knowing exactly what one was up to.

And so it was with a certain feeling of trepidation that she followed him into the study after the meal was over.

The study was crammed with old game bags, muddy boots, stuffed foxes, guns and rods and whips. The vicar shoved aside the miscellaneous clutter on his desk and sat down.

'Well, Annabelle,' he said, turning in his chair and facing her. 'Off to join the world, hey?'

'Yes, papa.'

'See here. You're a trifle young to be thinking o'marriage. But I was never one for lookin' a gift horse in the mouth and that there Marquess of Brabington seemed to have a liking for you.'

'Indeed, papa?' said Annabelle primly. 'I had not noticed.'

'No?' The vicar's gaze suddenly became very sharp. 'You ain't got any silly notions into that brain box o' yours, hey? Ain't formed a *tendre* for Comfrey?'

'Lord Sylvester? No,' said Annabelle faintly, glad that she was not blushing.

'If you say so. Gels at your age get these fancies for an older man sometimes. He's thirty-four.'

'He's not too old for Minerva.'

'No. Cos she's matured and you ain't. She spoiled you, you know. You were only sixteen when you were canoodling in the six acre with Guy Wentwater. Aye, that brings you to the blush. Didn't know I knew about *that*!'

'Mr Wentwater was merely expressing his affection, and, furthermore, I have not heard from him since.'

'Nor are like to,' said the vicar grimly.

'You did something to frighten him away,' exclaimed Annabelle.

'Not I,' said the vicar, looking the picture of innocence,

16

and mentally reminding the Almighty that it was sometimes politic to lie.

'Anyways,' he went on severely, 'I want you to behave yourself. No flashing your eyes and ogling the fellows, mind!'

'Papa!'

'And you will mind Minerva at all times. She's got her head screwed on the right way and you ain't.'

'Yes, papa,' said Annabelle through thin lips.

'And if you make any mischief, I shall get to hear of it and I'll take the horsewhip to you which is a thing I've had a mind to do many's a time, but Minerva always stepped in an' stopped me.'

'You would not *dare*!' gasped Annabelle. 'I, sir, am a lady.'

'That remains to be seen,' said the vicar calmly. 'I'm warning you, Annabelle, you keep your conversation civil and your manner modest.'

'Very well, papa.'

''Abstain from fleshly lusts, which war against the soul. Peter 1, Chapter 8, verse 11.'

'*Yes*, papa.'

'Now, here's a purse for you. Pin money and money for the servants. Off to bed with you.'

Folding her lips into a mutinous line, Annabelle stalked up the stairs to her room.

Deirdre was sitting at the toilet table, trying various creams on her face.

Annabelle's temper erupted and she ran at her younger sister and shook her till her teeth rattled.

'Get to your own room,' she hissed.

Deirdre wriggled out of Annabelle's grasp and danced to the door. 'You haven't a hope of Lord Sylvester even *looking* at you, Bella. Fair haired women aren't fashionable.'

'Neither are carrot tops,' screamed Annabelle. She seized a hair brush and threw it at her sister, but Deirdre quickly nipped around the door and was gone.

'Spiteful little *cat*!' muttered Annabelle, sitting down at

17

the toilet table and anxiously studying her reflection in the glass. Anger had brought a flush to her cheeks and a sparkle to her large blue eyes. Her blonde hair, which she still wore down, formed a golden aureole about her pretty face.

'I'm beautiful,' said Annabelle defiantly. 'Much more beautiful than Minerva.' Then suffocating excitement began to rise in her throat. Soon she would see Lord Sylvester. She began to weave rosy fantasies of returning to the vicarage with a doting Lord Sylvester on her arm and savoured the thought of Deirdre's consternation. 'This is my little sister,' she would say, patting Deirdre's hair. 'We must do something to reform her, darling. So wild in her ways, she will *never* catch a beau.'

But it was a rather small and scared and schoolgirlish Annabelle who bade farewell to her parents and sisters on the following day. The girls had been kept from school especially to say goodbye to her. The vicar promised to write to the twins that very day and tell them of Annabelle's visit to the Duke of Allsbury.

The magnificent glass-wigged coachman, grander than an archbishop, cracked his whip. Annabelle leaned out of the carriage window, seeing her family through a blur of tears. Two tall footmen jumped on the backstrap, the housemaid Betty clasped her hands in sheer ecstasy at the glory of the soft leather upholstery, the bearskin rugs, and the hot brick at her feet – and they were off.

'G-Goodbye,' choked Annabelle, fluttering her handkerchief. 'Oh, I *will* be good, papa.'

But the vicar's startled shout of, 'You weren't setting out to be anything else, were you?' was drowned in the rumble of the wheels.

Annabelle sat back in the corner and dried her streaming eyes. Was this how Minerva felt? she thought uneasily. Was this how she felt when she set out to London with instructions to find a husband? And wasn't it monstrous wicked even to think of depriving her of her

18

catch?

The coach rumbled on down through the village, casting its reflection in the still waters of the village pond, the four great horses pulling it sending out snorts of smoky breath into the frigid air.

Past the Six Jolly Beggarmen; past the wrinkled little figure of Squire Radford who raised his hat.

And on past the gates of The Hall, home of Annabelle's uncle, Sir Edwin Armitage. Sir Edwin, the vicar's brother, and his wife, Lady Edwin, had had their noses quite put out of joint by Minerva's success on the marriage mart. Their conceited daughters, Emily and Josephine, had not taken at all, and were all set to try again at the next Season.

At the thought of Josephine and Emily, Annabelle's uneasy conscience fled to be replaced by a rosy fantasy of presenting Lord Sylvester to them as *her* fiancé and watching the look on their Friday-faces.

The carriage swayed over the hump-backed bridge that spanned the River Blyne, and sent echoes flying back from the high mossy walls around Lady Wentwater's estate.

By the time the coach had swung out on to the Hopeminster Road, Annabelle's fantasy had faded, and once again she began worrying about how she would behave at the Duke of Allsbury's.

She tried to reassure herself by remembering that she had been on visits to their neighbour, Lord Osbadiston, who had lived in rather a grand style before his debts had caught up with him. But she had gone there with her family, very much one of the children. Now, visiting a Duke was almost as good as visiting royalty. It was said the Duke and Duchess of Allsbury held very fashionable house parties. Mrs Armitage would not have felt intimidated. She was so determined to prove that she was an ailing invalid that she did not really notice much of what was going on around her. Minerva, with a London Season behind her, would be quite at ease, but here Annabelle frowned. If she were to impress and charm Lord Sylvester, then she did not want to hide behind her sister's skirts.

If only she did not have to meet these mysterious young men! And if Minerva found them suitable, they must be boring in the extreme, thought Annabelle, determined to hang on to the idea that Minerva's engagement to Lord Sylvester had been a result of a temporary mental aberration on the part of that gentleman.

'Oh, Miss Bella,' cried the maid, Betty, breaking in to her thoughts. 'Ain't it scary to be visiting a real live dook?'

'You must learn to know your place, Betty,' said Annabelle severely, 'and call me Miss Annabelle from now on.'

'Yes'm,' said Betty with a little toss of her head. It was Miss Bella who would soon find she didn't know her place, thought Betty gleefully. And *that* would be fun to watch. Too full of herself was our Miss Bella!

CHAPTER TWO

After two days of travelling, Annabelle arrived at Haeter Abbey on a cold grey morning, with black massed clouds threatening snow.

She had expected a palace like Blenheim and experienced a sharp pang of disappointment as Haeter Abbey hove into view. It seemed a large, rather ugly house set in a flat park. In 1758, the young architect, Robert Adam, had designed the interiors, but by the time he had shown his plans for remodelling the outside of the building, the duke at that time had remarked curtly that he had spent enough money, and so the dull bare brick front with its squat row of columns stayed as it was.

The inside was another story. But, at first at least, Annabelle did not even notice its magnificence.

She was ushered into a large hall and stood hesitantly on its broad expanse of black and white tile. Adam's cool colours set off the Roman statuary which surrounded the room. At the end, a double flight of stairs curved up to the state rooms on the first floor.

Annabelle saw none of this magnificence. She dimly saw Minerva, her arms stretched out in welcome. But clear and sharp, she saw the tall, elegant figure of Lord Sylvester and hurtled towards it.

Throwing her arms around him, she turned her glowing face up to his. If ever a girl was waiting to be kissed, it was Annabelle.

Lord Sylvester Comfrey gave her cheek a careless flick of his hand and then gently disengaged himself.

'Welcome, Miss Annabelle,' he said. 'Your sister is waiting to greet you.'

Annabelle flushed delicately, realizing her mistake. Of course dear Sylvester would not show any unnecessary warmth in front of Minerva.

'I am *so* sorry, Lord Sylvester,' she said. 'You must think the long journey has addled my wits. I simply rushed into the arms of the first person I saw. Merva, it is *so* good to see you.'

She hugged and kissed her sister, noticing out of the corner of one blue eye that the rather blank look had left Lord Sylvester's green eyes and he was surveying her approvingly.

As she drew back, Annabelle was still so intent on charming Lord Sylvester that she did not notice Minerva's rather heightened colour.

'Come and I will take you to your room, Annabelle,' said Minerva, 'and we can have a comfortable coze. Lord Sylvester will excuse us.'

She put her arm around Annabelle's waist and led her up the stairs.

Annabelle was only dimly aware of a glory of rich colours and ornaments and paintings. She half turned on the landing and glanced down into the hall. A footman carrying a large candelabra was crossing it, but, of Lord Sylvester, there was no sign.

The bedroom allotted to Annabelle had a sitting room leading from it and a powder closet which had been turned into a small dressing room. The rooms were decorated in rich golds and crimsons with a seventeenth century tapestry depicting the death of Remus along one wall of the bedroom.

Annabelle rattled on breathlessly about the doings of the parish while Minerva helped Betty to unpack.

Then she changed out of her boots into a pair of beaded slippers and warmed her toes at the hearth. For the first time she looked fully at Minerva and felt a pang of sheer jealousy.

Minerva was wearing a classical, high-waisted, vertical gown with a high neck and deep muslin ruff in palest pink. The untrained skirt was ankle length with a slightly flared hem ornamented with Spanish trimmings. The sleeves were long and close fitting, ending in a muslin wrist frill. Her black hair was dressed *à la Titus*, artistically dishevelled curls springing from a centre parting. Her large grey eyes seemed almost silver and her cheeks were faintly flushed.

'You make me feel like a yokel,' said Annabelle with a rather shrill laugh. 'Mama said you would lend me some gowns, Merva. Please let me look at your wardrobe. I must look my best. And who are these gentlemen you wish me to meet?'

Minerva dismissed Betty to the servants quarters, softly closed the door behind the maid, and came and sat down opposite Annabelle, looking rather grave.

'Yes, you may choose any of my dresses you please,' said Minerva, 'and I shall tell you about the other guests shortly. But first I must explain something to you. The ways of the *haut ton* are not so very different from our ways. To be modest and pleasing at all times and not to talk too much are some necessary things to remember.'

Here Annabelle sighed loudly and tapped her foot impatiently on the fender.

'Don't prose so, Merva,' said Annabelle.

'Neither Mama nor Papa is here, so I stand in their place,' said Minerva severely. 'I must, therefore, tell you that your behaviour on arrival was disgraceful.'

'You refine too much upon it,' said Annabelle hotly. 'I *explained*. I was delighted to have arrived safely after a tedious journey. Sylvester is to be my brother-in-law ...'

'*Lord* Sylvester to you, miss.'

Annabelle suddenly grinned. 'You're jealous, Merva,' she said.

'No,' said Minerva coldly, 'you do me an injustice. Where Lord Sylvester is concerned, I have nothing to be jealous about.'

Minerva seemed so utterly sure of herself, so completely serene, that Annabelle experienced her first qualm of doubt. Could Lord Sylvester really love Minerva?

'You are very young, Bella,' said Minerva. 'Perhaps I was wrong to arrange this invitation for you.'

'No!' exclaimed Annabelle breathlessly, realizing she had gone too far. Memory of the vicar's threat of a horse whipping came back. 'I am really sorry I behaved in such a hoydenish way, Merva. Please say you forgive me.'

Now, the old Minerva would promptly have looked noble and accepted the apology on the spot. But this new, poised, strangely different sister only replied, 'Well, we shall see how

23

you go on. You wished to know about the young gentlemen. They are all a trifle too old for you, being in their twenties, but I thought it would be an opportunity for you to study how the other young ladies behave.'

'*Other* young ladies?'

'Yes, we are not without competition,' smiled Minerva. 'I had better tell you the names of everyone you are to meet. There is, of course, the Duke and Duchess of Allsbury. Lord Sylvester's older brother, the Marquess, is travelling in Russia and will not be with us. Then there are two cousins, the Misses Margaret and Belinda Forbes-Jydes; Lady Godolphin, of whom you have heard; Lady Coombes, a most elegant lady who is a relative; Sally and Betty Abernethy, Scotch ladies who are related to the Duchess's family, and that makes up the female side of the party.

'The gentlemen consist of a Colonel Arthur Brian who is by way of being a friend of Lady Godolphin.' Here Minerva's lips pressed into a severe disapproving line and Annabelle wondered why. 'Then there is the Honourable Harry Comfrey with his brother, Charles, both cousins, Lord Paul Chester, a friend of Lord Sylvester, as is Mr John Frampton ... oh, and I had almost forgot, the most exciting guest of all arrives tomorrow.'

'Who ...?'

'Why, Peter, Marquess of Brabington.'

'But why is that exciting? He is a very fine gentleman but ...'

'Do but listen! He is a hero! He sailed from Portsmouth shortly after we last saw him at the vicarage to rejoin his regiment in the Peninsula. But shortly out of Portsmouth, the ship, the *Mary Belle*, was hit with a mighty storm and the men had to take to the boats. The *Mary Belle* sank very rapidly and a deal of men were struggling in the water, and Lord Brabington who was on one of the long boats, kept going back and back, time after time, into that dreadful sea.

'It is estimated he saved the lives of ten men before he collapsed with exhaustion. He contracted a fever and is being brought here to rest until he is well again. He will be too weak to do little more than keep to his bed but we are all agog to welcome him.'

'He is a very brave man,' said Annabelle sincerely.

'Ah, yes,' laughed Minerva, 'I noticed that he was quite taken with you, Bella.'

'Really!' said Annabelle, affecting a yawn. 'How old is he?'

'I believe Sylvester said he had thirty years.'

'Oh, Merva. And you just said the gentlemen in their twenties were too old for me!' teased Annabelle.

'Well, if one meets an ... an older man who is out of the common way then such a difference in age does not matter.'

'No! It did not stop you from becoming engaged to Lord Sylvester despite a difference of fourteen years. But I forget. You were not looking for a love match. It was necessary for you to marry *anyone* with money to save our fortunes and I think it was all very noble of you, Merva.'

'I was not noble at all,' laughed Minerva. 'It is a love match.'

Annabelle's heart fell. But Minerva did not look like a woman in love. And she would say such a thing because it would not be right to say otherwise. So Annabelle tried to console herself.

As one grows older, the difference in ages seems to narrow. Someone of forty-five will feel on equal terms with someone of sixty. But between seventeen and twenty yawns a large gulf. Annabelle was still an adolescent girl while Minerva had become a woman. Added to that, Minerva had acted as substitute mother to the Armitage children, Mrs Armitage being too taken up with practising to be an invalid. One does not think at seventeen of one's mother having ever endured the burning fires of love, and so Annabelle could not bring herself to think that her aloof sister had ever felt the tremblings of passion. Nothing is more intense, or more self-centred than calf love.

Annabelle became aware that Minerva was speaking. 'We are to join the Duchess for luncheon. We have breakfast, luncheon and dinner here, quite like London. We do not sit down to dinner until eight o'clock in the evening! I shall lend you something grand for evening but we are quite informal for luncheon. Betty has laid out your pretty blue muslin.'

But Annabelle immediately pouted. 'Lend me one of yours, *please*,' she wheedled.

Visions of Lord Sylvester, waiting below at the luncheon table crowded into her mind. She could almost hear his mocking voice, see his beautifully sculptured mouth.

'No,' said Minerva firmly. 'There will not be ...'

'I don't *want* to wear that old blue thing,' said Annabelle, her voice rising. 'It's just like you to want to keep all the finest things for yourself.'

'That is unkind,' said Minerva. 'What has come over you, Annabelle?'

'I'm sorry,' said Annabelle, bursting into tears. 'But I do so want to look fashionable.'

She is still such a child, thought Minerva indulgently.

'There now,' she said. 'Dry your eyes. You may choose any gown you want.'

'Really? Anything?'

'Anything at all.'

'Oh, *thank* you!' cried Annabelle, her tears miraculously disappearing.

'Then come with me.'

An hour later, Annabelle was ready to descend the stairs. She had chosen a morning dress, with an apron front and stomacher let in and laced across like a peasant's bodice with coloured ribbons. It was made of jaconet muslin, white with a small design in cherry red, and with cherry red silk ribbons.

Her blonde hair had been put up in a loose knot on the top of her head, allowing a cascade of ringlets to fall to her shoulders. Minerva thought Annabelle had never looked more beautiful – and Annabelle thought so too.

It was with great bitterness that Annabelle found she was to waste all this sweetness on the desert air.

Luncheon was to be served in the Yellow Saloon on the ground floor, a pretty room affording an excellent view of the park.

But it was the sight of the company that depressed Annabelle so. There were no gentlemen present, and, worst of all, certainly no Lord Sylvester.

The company for luncheon consisted only of the Duchess of Allsbury and Lady Godolphin.

The Duchess was a small, plump lady with beautifully dressed white hair and large green eyes which had faded with age to a sort of pale gooseberry colour. She had an easy outer manner covering a rather frosty interior. In truth, her grace privately disapproved of her youngest son's forthcoming marriage to Minerva Armitage, thinking he was throwing himself away by affiancing himself to some little nobody from a country vicarage. But Minerva, in her way, could be almost as intimidating as Lord Sylvester, and so she had kept her thoughts to herself. It would certainly be understandable if she had disapproved of Lady Godolphin, but Lady Godolphin came from a very old family, and so the Duchess found nothing up with that reprehensible old quiz.

Annabelle had not really been warned about Lady Godolphin since she had not quite taken in her mother's remarks, and Minerva would have considered it disloyal to criticize the lady who had been her chaperone.

Lady Godolphin was a squat lady in her late fifties with a bulldog face and pale blue eyes. She wore a great deal of pearl powder over a covering of white lead paint. Two round circles of rouge glared from her withered cheeks and a scarlet wig perched at an improbable angle on her head.

She was wearing a very low cut gown of acid green velvet and the ageing flesh of her breasts quivered under their coating of white lead every time she moved like the winter water shivering under a coating of thin ice on the lake outside.

Lady Godolphin sprang to her feet at their entrance, and, without waiting to be introduced, enfolded Annabelle in a warm and smelly embrace. Annabelle extricated herself as soon as she decently could, noticing as she did so that some of her ladyship's white paint had smeared the cherry red ribbons of her bodice.

'Ain't you the pretty one,' crowed Lady Godolphin. 'You'll have all the fellows shaking in their shoes like blankmanjies. I don't know how Charles Armitage

27

produced such beauties. He's so obesed with the chase, one would expect him to have sired a pack o' fox-faced long-nosed antidotes.'

'Where are the gentlemen, my lady?' asked Annabelle, looking anxiously at the four settings on the table and wishing there were more so she might at least *hope*.

'Gone out riding with the ladies,' said the Duchess calmly. 'Pray be seated, Miss Annabelle. I trust your journey was not too fatiguing? No? Good. That is a pretty gown you are wearing.'

'I remember it well,' said Lady Godolphin, as they all seated themselves at the table. 'I bought it for Minerva. It's as well you are of a size and you ain't too proud to wear hand-me-downs.'

Annabelle's glorious beauty seemed to pale and fade under the mortification inflicted by these words. But the thought that this amiable-looking Duchess might one day be her mother-in-law stiffened her spine, and she contented herself with smiling vaguely at some point over Lady Godolphin's shoulder.

The Duchess launched into a conversation with Lady Godolphin of the do-you-know and how-are-the-so-and-sos variety while Minerva and Annabelle were obliged to sit mum and behave like good little girls.

Annabelle gamely, at one point, tried to break in by saying to the Duchess, 'You have a beautiful house,' but her grace only fixed her with a pleasant smile which did not quite reach her eyes, replied, 'Yes,' and continued to talk to Lady Godolphin.

After some time the Duchess asked Lady Godolphin, 'And how goes Mr Brummell? Still ruling the roost?'

Annabelle immediately pricked up her ears for Lady Godolphin's reply, for Mr George Brummell *was* fashion. It was said the Prince Regent had blubbered like a baby when Mr Brummell had criticized the cut of his coat.

'Oh, tol rol,' said Lady Godolphin, waving her pudgy fingers in a dismissive kind of way. 'He still works so hard at being the fashion which, of course, anyone with a doubtful pedigree must do. He toadies very cleverly when he is not being frightfully rude and they all love him for it. Like those women who like being insulted by their hairdresser. It appeals to their love of dollar and humiliation.'

There was a little silence while the other three ladies tried to think what Lady Godolphin could possibly mean by 'love of dollar'.

It was rather like doing an acrostic, thought Annabelle.

'*Douleur*—the French for pain,' said Minerva suddenly, her face clearing.

Lady Godolphin nodded her large head. 'That's just what I said, Minerva. There's no need to go on repeating my words, you know. We ain't deaf.'

Annabelle and Minerva solemnly bowed their heads over their food.

At last, the meal was over and the two Armitage girls were free to make their escape.

'How *could* you bear being brought out by *her*,' whispered Annabelle as they were mounting the grand staircase. 'She is *awful*. And I don't think the Duchess likes us one bit.'

She expected this latter remark to shock Minerva for she had never thought her sister a very perceptive sort of girl, but Minerva said, 'I will not have to see much of her once I am married ... the Duchess, that is. Lady Godolphin is quite shocking, I agree, but she has a very kind heart.'

'It's a wonder you noticed it,' said Annabelle acidly, 'hidden as it must be under at least three feet of *blanc*.'

'Hush!' said Minerva. 'We must not criticize our elders.'

'Oh, *Merva*, if you don't really think she's a frightful old hag then you are a hypocrite, or, as her ladyship would no doubt say, a hippopotamous.'

But Minerva was not to be drawn on the subject of Lady Godolphin. 'You must lie down and rest,' she told Annabelle. 'For they keep very late hours here. No! You must be guided by me. Off to bed!'

Rather sulkily, Annabelle complied, but no sooner was she in the privacy of her rooms than she was overcome by a fit of rebellion. 'Late hours' probably meant nine o'clock to Minerva. And why waste time sleeping when she could be on the watch for Lord Sylvester?

Finding the windows of her sitting room overlooked the main entrance, she settled down to wait.

Small flakes of snow, round and hard as pellets, were beginning to fall. Annabelle watched as the bare branches of the trees began to bend in the rising wind and the sky grew even darker above.

She stared down the long straight drive. At one moment, she would think she could see a party of riders, and then the next, would realize that the blowing, thickening snow was tricking her vision.

And then all at once they appeared, clattering up the drive, Lord Sylvester and a middle-aged woman in a smart frogged riding dress leading the way.

Annabelle sprang to her feet, and then stood irresolute. She did not want to confront all these strangers. At last she decided to creep quietly to the top of the stairs and see if she could find a chance to speak to Lord Sylvester when the others had retired to their rooms.

There was an alcove with a large bronze statue of Zeus on the first landing and Annabelle managed to hide behind it without being seen by any of the guests or servants.

Several young women and men mounted the stairs and passed her. After what seemed an unbearably long time, the middle-aged lady came up and walked past, holding the long train of her riding dress over one arm. She looked very elegant and *mondaine*. That must be Lady Coombes, thought Annabelle, remembering Minerva's description of the guests.

Then there was a long silence, punctuated only by faint sounds of voices and laughter from the rooms above.

Annabelle slipped quietly down the stairs to the main hall. The statues surrounding the hall seemed to watch her with their bronze eyes.

There were so many rooms. Where could he have gone? A butler wearing a green baize apron came into the hall and Annabelle flashed him a bright smile.

'Can you tell me the whereabouts of Lord Sylvester Comfrey?' she asked.

'In the library, miss,' replied the butler.

'Which is …?'

'Over there, miss, at the far end of the hall on the right.'

Annabelle's heart began to beat hard and she felt a suffocating constriction at her chest. For one desperate moment she wanted to turn and flee, but the butler was standing gravely watching her so she put up her chin and marched to the back of the hall.

Gently she pushed open the library door and walked inside. Lord Sylvester was standing over at one of the long windows, a calf-bound volume in his hand. He was wearing a dark forest green coat over a short waistcoat of printed marseilles, kerseymere breeches and brown top boots. His light brown hair was artistically arranged as if he had just left the hands of the hairdresser. He did not look up as Annabelle entered, seeming totally immersed in his book.

'One would not think you had just been out riding,' said Annabelle in a breathless voice. 'You look as if you had just stepped out of a bandbox.'

Lord Sylvester lowered his book and turned and looked at Annabelle, his green eyes totally expressionless.

'I beg your pardon, Miss Annabelle,' he said languidly. 'I did not hear what you said.'

'I-I said you looked as if you had stepped from a bandbox instead of having been out riding,' repeated Annabelle weakly. 'I-I m-mean in this weather.'

'Indeed?' His lordship stood calmly surveying her, obviously waiting for her to go on.

'There are a lot of books here,' said Annabelle.

'Yes. We are in the library.'

'Do you read much?'

'When I am allowed time to do so … yes.'

'I … I read a lot too.'

'Then you are in the right place,' said his lordship blandly, tucking his book under one arm and making for the door. 'You will find something to suit your taste, I am sure.'

'Wait!' said Annabelle desperately. Had he not noticed how fine she looked in the gown with the cherry ribbons? 'Perhaps you could suggest something …?'

'No. I could not. I do not know your taste.'

'Oh. Well ... well then ... you see it is so *strange* here.'

His face relaxed and he smiled. 'I am surprised my conscientious Minerva left you to your own devices.'

'Yes, she *is* very severe, isn't she?' said Annabelle with a giggle. 'Does she bully you too?'

'Oh, yes, quite dreadfully. But you have not answered my question.'

'Minerva thinks I am lying down having a rest.'

'And you could not?' said Lord Sylvester, making a half turn towards the door.

'No. I was too excited. And I wanted to see you.'

'Here I am. And here I go. Old fogies like me need our rest, Miss Annabelle.'

'You are not *at all* old,' said Annabelle, her eyes glowing. 'I *like* mature gentlemen.'

'Thank you. I am glad I find favour in the eyes of my future sister-in-law. Now if you will ...'

'And ... and ... the men I have met have been so *dull*.'

'There are many charming young men here, and you will meet them all this evening.'

'What is that you are reading?' asked Annabelle, coming to stand close to him.

'Ovid's *Metamorphoses*.'

'May I see it?'

'As you wish.' Lord Sylvester held out the book to her and Annabelle looked down at the musty pages in an unseeing kind of way, racking her brains to say something that would keep him.

Suddenly she hit upon an idea. 'Will there be dancing this evening?' she asked, turning a glowing face up to his.

'Very possibly. After dinner. We often have dancing and cards when we have guests.'

Annabelle took a deep breath.

'And will you dance with me?'

'Yes I will dance with you, my child,' he said, taking her hand and kissing it. 'And now I must go.'

Annabelle stood alone in the library for a long time after he had left, holding the hand he had kissed to her cheek and staring out at the falling snow.

She had been right! He had noticed her. His feelings towards her were warm or he would not have kissed her hand. She turned their conversation over and over in her mind, reading into every casual answer a double meaning, into every polite and bored gesture, hints of a growing passion being held well in check.

At last, she returned dreamily to her room, building dream upon dream, fantasy upon fantasy, so that when Minerva and her maid eventually arrived with their arms full of dresses for her to choose from, Annabelle could only look at her sister with a sort of awkward pity, already imagining the engagement to be broken.

Despite protests from Minerva that her choice of gown was 'a trifle old' for her, Annabelle insisted on wearing a gown of sage-green China crêpe, brocaded in stripes. It had the fashionable high waist and low bosom. Her one piece of jewellery, a necklace of garnets, was clasped around her neck. Minerva had to admit the finished effect was breathtaking. But Minerva had always considered Annabelle to be the beauty of the family, unaware that her own appearance in a white slip covered with soft grey gauze and with a simple string of pearls around her neck made her the more elegant beauty of the two.

The Armitage sisters caused a small sensation when they walked into the Long Gallery where all the other guests were already assembled.

They were the last to arrive, Annabelle having changed her mind several times at the last minute over the choice of a fan.

The Misses Margaret and Belinda Forbes-Jydes were, Annabelle was pleased to note, nothing out of the common way, being both very short and having an unfortunate colour of sandy hair. Sally and Betty Abernethy were more handsome, but Annabelle's quick eyes at last remarked that Miss Sally had a slight cast in one eye, and that Miss Betty had a flat bosom. Lady Coombes was handsome in a severe way, with black and grey hair exquisitely dressed. The Duchess and Lady Godolphin were sitting chatting in a corner, Lady Godolphin wearing the most hideous turban Annabelle had ever seen.

She tried hard not to stare at Lord Sylvester and studied the other gentlemen.

The Duke of Allsbury, unlike his son, was short and tubby with a high, red colour and enormous cavalry whiskers. The other elderly gentleman with his face stained with walnut juice to a mahogany colour was Colonel Arthur Brian. The Honourable Harry Comfrey and his brother, Charles, were both stocky young men, both wearing cravats tied in the Oriental, which meant they could barely turn their heads. Lord Paul Chester was an elegantly dressed, vague young man with butter-coloured hair cut in a fashionable Brutus crop, and Mr John Frampton was a tall, handsome man with brown hair and twinkling blue eyes. Mindful that the two latter gentlemen were friends of Lord Sylvester, Annabelle set herself to please. This she did by asking a deal of intelligent questions, listening politely and carefully, and not talking overmuch herself. After a few anxious moments, Minerva decided Annabelle was behaving very well indeed and went to join her fiancé.

'Is not Annabelle in looks?' she asked.

Lord Sylvester put up his quizzing glass and studied Annabelle, who had managed to attract the four young gentlemen of the company to her side.

'She is very beautiful,' he said, letting his glass fall. 'Unfortunately, that is a fact of which she is well aware.'

'You are too harsh, my love. She is very young.'

Lord Sylvester smiled down at Minerva. 'When you call me "my love", all I can think of is that it is too long since I held you in my arms.'

'I kissed you last night,' said Minerva blushing rosily.

'I was thinking of something more intimate.'

Minerva blushed deeper. 'I feel what we did that night was a sin,' she whispered. 'The circumstances were strange, dear Sylvester. I thought you were to be killed in a duel or I would *never* have ... never would ...'

'Oh, prim Minerva. Are you to keep me waiting until the wedding?'

34

'Yes ... no ... I don't know.'

A sudden overloud burst of laughter from Annabelle made Minerva swing around anxiously.

'That girl is *quite* uninhabited,' commented Lady Godolphin from close by.

At that moment, Annabelle caught her sister's reproving gaze and once more became the picture of a modest miss. But although she had been charming her small court to perfection, she had eagerly watched the exchange between Lord Sylvester and her sister out of the corner of her eye. They did not look like a couple in love, thought Annabelle, not knowing that Lord Sylvester's understated behaviour was, this time, very definitely covering the feelings of a man holding his passion in check.

Annabelle found to her disappointment that she was not to be seated next to Lord Sylvester at dinner. In fact, as the least distinguished of the guests, she was placed between Mr Charles Comfrey and Mr John Frampton.

But Mr Frampton was very handsome. Annabelle decided it would do no harm to see if she could make Lord Sylvester jealous. No allowance had been made for her youth and so wine had been put in front of her instead of lemonade.

Annabelle had had occasional glasses of wine at high days and holidays, but this wine was heavily fortified with brandy. Added to that, the fatigue of her journey now hit her, and she began to feel very elated, very fascinating, and very beautiful. She basked in the warm admiration of Mr Frampton's eyes and barely listened to what he was saying until something caught her attention. Mr Frampton was talking about his young brother at Cambridge who had done exceptionally well in his examinations.

Here, Annabelle decided, was an opportunity to try out some of that delicious slang.

'I have a friend at College,' she said airily. 'The nask, he calls it. He pays chummage, you know, so that he can get a room to himself. Not that he had much money. I told him not to play in that low dive. That Greek ivory turner

35

used a bale of bard cinque deuces on him so it's all Dicky with poor Barry.'

There was a stunned silence. Mr Frampton took out a large pocket handkerchief and appeared to blow his nose. At last he emerged from behind it and said in a stifled voice, 'Dear me, do you have *many* friends in prison, Miss Annabelle?'

'I don't understand,' said Annabelle blankly.

He looked down at her, his blue eyes twinkling. 'Do you know what you have just said?'

'Of course!'

'Well, let's suppose you don't. You said you have a friend who is in the nask, or College, which is underworld cant for prison. I assume he landed there by getting into debt after playing with loaded dice in a gambling hell. Paying chummage is the only way you can get a room to yourself in some prisons – that is you pay your two cell mates, or chums, a certain amount of money to sleep on the stairs. And as for saying it's all Dicky – oh, Miss Armitage, I do *hope* you don't know what that means but I can only beg you never to use that expression again.'

He gave her a sympathetic smile and then turned to talk to Sally Abernethy on his other side.

Annabelle sat very still, her face scarlet. It took her some time to realize that Mr Charles Comfrey on her other side had plunged into speech, but after a little while of appearing to listen to him, she managed to regain her composure.

So well did she manage that when Mr Frampton turned back to her she was able to say with every appearance of ease, 'You must excuse me, Mr Frampton. My wicked tongue does run away with me. I was merely funning. I do apologize.'

'Your apology is accepted,' he smiled. 'I am really quite unshockable, you know. And you had me well and truly fooled for I thought you were in earnest. Never did I think to hear such words issuing from such a beautiful pair of lips.'

'Mr Frampton!' protested Annabelle, raising her fan

and flirting with her large blue eyes over the top of it. 'Now *you* shock *me!*'

They settled down to a light flirtation which lasted so pleasantly throughout the rest of the meal that Annabelle drank a great deal more wine without being at all aware of what she was doing.

From where she sat at the far end of the table, Minerva could not see her sister and assumed all was well.

When the ladies retired to the Long Gallery to leave the gentlemen to their wine, Annabelle wandered off by herself to study the family portraits, standing with her hands behind her back and looking so like a well-behaved child that Minerva settled down beside the Duchess, feeling quite at ease.

It was only when the gentlemen joined the ladies that Minerva began to feel there was something amiss.

Annabelle, not to put too fine a point on it, began to show off disgracefully. Minerva could not hear what she was saying because the Duchess was prosing on about curtain material, but she could tell by the sight of her sister's waving arms and flushed face that Annabelle was getting above herself.

She looked up and caught Lord Sylvester's eye and gave a desperate little signal for help, nodding in Annabelle's direction.

Lord Sylvester strolled up to the group of four gentlemen and five ladies who were surrounding Annabelle.

As he arrived, the Duchess finished talking, Minerva was watching Annabelle anxiously, and, in the silence, Mr Charles Comfrey said, 'I say, do you think Brummell will approve of this green coat of mine if I sport it at Almack's or will he give me one of his famous set downs?'

And clear as a bell, Annabelle's overloud voice resounded around the Long Gallery. 'Oh, you must be careful,' she laughed. 'No gentleman wears green any more. It is so terribly Old Hat.'

There was a stunned silence.

'DIS*graceful!*' snapped Lady Coombes turning on her

37

heel and walking away.

The young ladies looked blank. Mr Frampton turned away to hide his laughter, Mr Charles Comfrey looked stricken, Mr Harry Comfrey muttered, 'Good Gad,' Lord Paul Chester raised his quizzing glass and studied Annabelle curiously as if he had just discovered some rare type of cockroach, and Lord Sylvester walked forwards with his charming smile and said, 'I think we should have some dancing to please the ladies. I have promised Miss Annabelle the first.'

Annabelle gratefully took his arm. She was aware she had said something dreadfully wrong, but Lord Sylvester's suggestion was immediately hailed by cries of pleasure from the ladies. His mother, explained Lord Sylvester, had hired musicians for the evening.

At that moment, the musicians were ushered in through a door at the far end and soon everyone with the exception of Lady Godolphin and Minerva and Colonel Brian were busy performing a country dance.

'What did my sister say that was so wrong?' said Minerva to Lady Godolphin.

'I ain't telling you,' said that lady roundly. 'I wouldn't soil my lips.'

'Oh, dear,' said Minerva sadly.

'Furthermore, she looks downright boosey to me,' said Lady Godolphin. 'Better get her off to bed as soon as this set is over.'

Minerva waited as patiently as she could. The dance was at last over and Annabelle sank in a deep curtsey in front of Lord Sylvester and then found she could not get up.

He raised her to her feet and steadied her by putting an arm around her waist.

'Bed for you, Miss Annabelle,' he said.

'I must speak to you. When shall I see you?'

'Soon,' he replied mockingly.

'Where?'

'I shall know where to find you.'

And to Annabelle's tipsy mind that meant Lord

Sylvester had as good as made an assignation. She meekly allowed Minerva to lead her from the room. *He* would come to her later. He had said so.

Minerva looked at her sister's flushed face and drowsy eyes and decided to leave all lectures until the morning. Together with the maid, Betty, she got Annabelle to bed, comfortably sure that that infuriating miss would be fast asleep as soon as ever she tiptoed from the room.

But love is a wonderful thing. Tired as she was, tipsy as she was, no sooner had Minerva and the maid left than Annabelle sat up wide awake and trembling with anticipation and excitement.

Dreams of love and romance made the time go quickly, and quite an hour had passed when she suddenly looked down at the schoolgirlish cut of her nightgown and frowned. He should not find her like this. She would creep along to Minerva's room and choose a simply splendid nightgown. Minerva had already amassed most of her trousseau, or torso as that reprehensible old Mrs Malaprop, Lady Godolphin, had called it.

Minerva's room was situated some corridors away. Annabelle, not wanting to be found by the servants wandering about in her nightclothes, quietly put on a warm walking dress over her nightgown and made her way stealthily along to Minerva's rooms. The faint sounds of music and voices filtered from downstairs.

She went into Minerva's bedroom and began to search through her chest of drawers for something suitable to wear.

All at once, she heard voices in the corridor outside.

She froze with her hands still buried among the silks and lace.

Then to her horror, she heard the door of the sitting room next door opening and Minerva's voice saying, 'You may come in, but just for a moment, Sylvester. I must know what it was she said.'

Heart beating hard, Annabelle moved swiftly behind the bedroom door which was standing open and found that by putting her eye to the hinge, she could see clearly into the lamplit sitting room next door.

Lord Sylvester and Minerva were standing facing each other in front of the fireplace.

'What did Annabelle say that was so wrong?' asked Minerva plaintively.

'Young Charles Comfrey was talking about that green coat of his and wondering whether he should sport it at Almack's during the coming Season or whether it would bring down one of Brummell's acid remarks on his head if he did so. Your sister said, if I remember aright, "No gentleman wears green anymore. It is so terribly Old Hat." '

'Well,' came Minerva's puzzled voice. 'Surely she meant that green coats are not fashionable any more.'

'I am sure she did, my sweeting, but Old Hat is cant, and that is not what the expression means.'

'Then what does it mean?'

'To put it bluntly, it means a woman's privities.'

'A woman's … but why Old Hat?'

'Because both, my love, are frequently felt.'

Minerva raised her hands to her suddenly scarlet cheeks, unaware that in the next room her sister was doing exactly the same thing.

'I *must* speak to her, Sylvester,' wailed Minerva. 'Your mother does not approve of me and *now* what will she think.'

'Minerva,' said Lord Sylvester patiently, 'You should know by now I do not give a rap what anyone thinks, least of all my mother. So kiss me, Minerva, and let's forget about that tiresome child.'

'But Sylvester, I …'

In front of Annabelle's horrified and humiliated eyes, Lord Sylvester bent his head and ruthlessly and savagely began to kiss Minerva.

One little hope kept Annabelle rooted to the spot. The prim Minerva would surely cry out against such an embrace.

Lord Sylvester finally drew back and smiled tenderly into Minerva's eyes.

'Well ..?' he whispered.

Hypnotized, Annabelle watched as Minerva's little hands went up to Lord Sylvester's cravat and slowly began to undo it.

She gave a choked little sound, and, moving like a sleepwalker, she went to the door of the sitting room and gently let herself out and closed the door just as gently behind her. Moving one foot carefully in front of the other, feeling her way along like Madame Saqui ascending the slack-rope at Vauxhall Gardens, she finally gained the security of her own rooms. She laid herself carefully down on top of the bed, closed her eyes, and plunged immediately into sleep, putting away all the pain and humiliation till the morrow.

CHAPTER THREE

The morning dawned white and cold with snow waves covering the Park. Annabelle lay in bed, very still, staring up at the canopy. Her soul felt as white and numb and empty as the day outside. Somewhere at the very edges of her mind she knew that pain and humiliation were waiting to crowd in. But, for the moment, all she wanted to do was lie very still and think of absolutely nothing.

Betty came in with her morning chocolate and drew the curtains, filling the room with white light. Soon the fire was crackling in the hearth. Annabelle caught the look that Betty threw in her direction: sly, gleeful, full of recently relayed gossip.

The maid went out and Annabelle wearily sat up. She felt she had not slept at all. Then it all came crushing back in a great red wave of pain.

Minerva. Prim, staid, correct Minerva untying Lord Sylvester's cravat. The passionate embrace. Clear as a bell, Lord Sylvester's voice sounded in her brain: 'So kiss me, Minerva, and let's forget about that tiresome child.'

Annabelle writhed in an agony of humiliation. She *could not* dress and go downstairs. How they would all laugh. How that terrible Duchess would gloat and tell everyone that the Armitage family was as common as a barber's chair.

But slowly, somewhere at the very depths of her misery, a little spark of anger took light and slowly grew into a flame. Minerva had always been the loved one, Minerva was always the good one. Oh, to steal some of Minerva's thunder.

There was a commotion below the windows and the sound of voices.

Annabelle suddenly swung her legs over the bed, glancing as she did so at the clock on the mantel.

Eleven o'clock!

Shivering in the still chilly room although she was still wearing her dress over her nightgown, she looked out of the window.

The Marquess of Brabington was being helped down from a travelling carriage by two strong footmen. Although she could see little more than the top of his hat, Annabelle knew it was he by his scarlet regimentals.

A small knot of people, including Lord Sylvester, surrounded him and then he was helped into the house.

Annabelle sat down on the edge of the bed and began to think furiously. The Marquess had shown more than a passing interest in her on the two occasions when he had called at the vicarage. He was a marquess, he was handsome, he was rich, and he was a hero. He was also Lord Sylvester's best friend.

'If I married him,' said Annabelle to the fire, 'then I should be a marchioness. And ... and ... I would suggest a double wedding, and wouldn't *that* take the wind out of Minerva's sails. Lord Sylvester is only a viscount so it means I would take precedence over Minerva at all the balls and parties. I should make him the happiest of men while Lord Sylvester becomes tired of his prosy wife. He *did* say Minerva bullied him. We should be accounted the most handsome pair in London.'

Annabelle's formidable vanity began to reassert itself. She rang the bell to summon Betty and curtly ordered the maid to lay out her grey gown, watching all the while for any signs of dumb insolence on Betty's part. But Betty had seen the militant look in Annabelle's eye and knew better than to do anything that might bring one of Miss Bella's famous tantrums down on her head. Betty was surprised at her mistress's choice of gown, knowing that Annabelle had threatened many a time to throw that 'dowdy Quakerish rag away'.

It was made of nankeen in the pelisse style with small raised buttons down the front from the high neck to the floor-length hem. The sleeves were long and close fitting to the wrist.

But Annabelle had a part to play and she meant to play it to the hilt. As soon as she had been helped into her underclothes and gown, she dismissed Betty, saying she would arrange her hair herself.

'Now,' thought Annabelle, sitting down at the toilet table and studying her wan face, 'I must look *reposeful* with a faint suggestion of the nurse.'

She brushed out her long blonde hair until it crackled, and then pinned it up in a knot on top of her head, letting only one curl escape.

Then she opened a small locked chest where, unbeknown to her parents, she kept her cosmetics.

Annabelle made better cosmetics than anyone between Hopeworth and Hopeminster and often earned pin money for herself by selling them to the women of the village.

She took out a stick of white grease paint and looked at it thoughtfully. She had made it with a mixture of prepared chalk, zinc oxide, bismuth subnitrate, asbestos powder, sweet almond oil, camphor, oil peppermint and esobouquet extract. Although she had experimented with it in the privacy of her bedchamber, she had never worn it in public.

Very cautiously and carefully, she applied it to her face, making sure not to put too much on. Popular rouges were bright red, dark red, and vermilion, but the skilful Annabelle had concocted herself a pale pink rouge.

Instead of painting a round circle on each cheek, she smoothed it on very carefully, blending it in with the white greasepaint. Then came the rose *poudre de riz* which she had made from cornstarch, powdered talc, oil of rose and extract of jasmine. She moved the haresfoot delicately over her skin, and then sat back and frowned at her reflection. Annabelle's lashes were as thick as Minerva's, but they were fair.

After some thought she took an orange stick, went over to one of the lamps and scraped off some of the lamp black, and then, returning to the looking glass, carefully applied the black to each lash until she was satisfied that they were dark enough to look natural, but not black

44

enough to look fake.

She heard a soft step in the corridor outside and hastily bundled her cosmetics back into their tin box and slammed down the lid just as Minerva came into the room.

'Oh, Annabelle,' said Minerva, forgetting for the moment the lecture she had come to deliver, 'I have never seen you in better looks. When you make your come-out, you will be the most beautiful girl London has ever seen!'

'Thank you,' said Annabelle, lowering her blackened eyelashes to mask a sudden spasm of irritation. Why must Minerva's praise always be so generous and unaffected? Surely she must feel just a *little* jealousy. Now she, Annabelle, was quite pleased to see that her sister was looking a trifle haggard and that she had dark circles under her eyes.

Then several crude and quite unmaidenly thoughts as to how Minerva came by those signs of fatigue flashed through her brain and she became more than ever determined to put Minerva's nose out of joint. Just let's see how sweet Minerva stayed when she realized her famous wedding was to be shared by her sister!

But there was one good thing. If Minerva had not noticed the paint and merely thought Annabelle's glowing complexion was the result of natural beauty, then so would everyone else.

Feeling composed, she raised her eyes to her sister and said quickly, 'Merva, I know you have come to scold me about last night. But what did I say that was so very wrong?'

'I asked Sylvester,' said Minerva, 'and you must understand that what you said – in all innocence – was in fact a piece of low cant which should never pass the lips of any lady. I am only glad you left the company so early. *That* at least shows some sense. I am sure everyone will realize that you were a trifle well to go, what with you not being used to so much wine or such late hours. Now I am not going to say any more ...'

'Good,' said Annabelle rudely.

45

'The Marquess of Brabington has arrived and we are all to take a little luncheon together so I am come to fetch you.'

'Then let us go,' said Annabelle, rising to her feet.

As they went downstairs, Annabelle turned over the events of the previous day, and by the time they reached the dining room, she was beginning to feel very ill-used.

Lord Sylvester had led her on, had *led* her to believe that his affections were not untouched. Had he not kissed her hand? And had he not said he would see her later?

At least I am now indifferent to him, thought Annabelle rather savagely.

But as they entered the dining room, her eyes flew immediately to the tall figure of Lord Sylvester and she was flooded with such a strong feeling of love and longing that she nearly gasped.

Now with her eyes sharpened with jealousy could Annabelle see the warmth and love in his green eyes as Lord Sylvester walked forwards to meet Minerva.

Tearing her gaze away from this painful sight, she found the Marquess of Brabington looking at her and dropped him a demure curtsey.

Why, she thought, this will not be so very bad after all.

She had forgotten that he was an extremely handsome man with his strong nose, cleft chin, thick black hair, and eyes of a peculiar tawny shade.

He was looking very pale. Then Annabelle became aware of an undercurrent of excitement in the room. All the ladies were chattering and talking gaily and from time to time their eyes would slide coyly in the direction of the handsome Marquess.

Everyone took their places around the table, Annabelle crossly noticing that Minerva was between the Marquess and Lord Sylvester while she herself was back with Mr Charles Comfrey and Mr John Frampton.

Since it was more breakfast than luncheon and not a formal meal, conversation went across the table instead of being confined to whoever was on one's right or one's left.

Lady Godolphin was seated opposite Annabelle,

wearing a nutty brown wig this time, and a more modest dress than she usually affected.

Annabelle poked at the dish of fish, eggs and rice in front of her.

'What is this?' asked Annabelle.

'Kennel grease,' replied Lady Godolphin. 'My favourite dish.'

'She means kedgeree,' whispered Mr Frampton in Annabelle's ear. 'My lady is in form this morning.'

Lady Godolphin kept staring at Annabelle in an unnerving way. She had decided that Annabelle wanted manners, and so, in between great mouthfuls of rice, she began to expound on the necessity of good behaviour in young ladies.

'When I was Minerva's chaperone,' said Lady Godolphin, 'I told her that I may have my prejuices, I may be too strict, but I can't abide Sophy Tray nor yet ladies without Property. Ladies without Property tie their garters in public, that they do, and Worse!'

'Propriety,' muttered Mr Frampton.

'Who is Sophy Tray?' asked Annabelle.

'Sophistry.'

'Ah.'

'And our handsome hero here,' went on Lady Godolphin, waving a forkful of rice in the direction of the Marquess, 'has set a few hearts a-flutter, but it ain't no use you young gels gettin' your hopes up. Everyone knows Lord Brabington to be a famous Missing Jest.'

'Do you mean that I am a poor sort of joke?' asked the Marquess with interest.

'I think my lady means misogynist,' said Minerva in rather governessy tones. 'Someone who does not like women.'

'That's what I *said*,' pointed out Lady Godolphin crossly. 'You'll need to take her in hand, Comfrey. Got a nasty habit of repeating what one says and translating as if one spoke behindy, as the Colonel here calls one of them Indian languages.'

'She really is impossible,' said Mr Comfrey to

47

Annabelle.

'Oh, Minerva is *always* like that,' said Annabelle sweetly. 'Poor Lord Sylvester. She will tell him from morn till night to mind his Ps and Qs.'

'I was referring to Lady Godolphin,' said Mr Comfrey, very stiffly on his stiffs. 'I would not dream of criticizing Miss Armitage. We all think Sylvester is a very lucky fellow. To be wedding all that beauty and maidenly modesty ... well, I just hope I am as fortunate.'

He turned away from Annabelle to speak to his neighbour and Annabelle cursed herself for having let her jealousy trip up her tongue. Of course she had known Mr Comfrey was referring to Lady Godolphin, but it was so maddening the way everyone admired Minerva. If they only knew what a *bore* she could be.

Mr Frampton then turned politely to tell her that the gentlemen were going out shooting that afternoon and asked whether the ladies had decided as to how they would spend their day.

'We have not yet had time,' replied Annabelle, thinking hard. 'I am surprised Lord Brabington should wish to engage in any form of sport after his ordeal.'

'I don't suppose Brabington will feel up to it,' replied Mr Frampton carelessly.

Just then, the Duchess's voice sounded down the table. 'The ladies have a treat in store for them this afternoon. While you gentlemen are floundering about in the snow with your guns, we shall be very cosy here. Lady Coombes has promised to show us her watercolour sketches of Wells Cathedral.'

There was a polite murmur from the ladies, the younger contingent trying to look pleased.

Annabelle then vowed to herself that whatever happened she was *not* going to spend the afternoon listening to Lady Coombes. The Marquess, provided he did not retire to his bedchamber, should be hunted down. There was no time to lose.

Annabelle was beginning to feel much better now that she had a plan of campaign in mind. And no one had commented on her horrible gaffe of the night before. No one seemed to remember it.

But in this, she was to be proved wrong. No sooner was breakfast over than the Duchess of Allsbury with a polite smile requested the presence of Miss Annabelle Armitage in the morning room for a few minutes.

'I will come too,' said Minerva quickly.

'No, my dear,' said the Duchess. 'What I have to say to Miss Annabelle must be said in private.'

A mutinous look began to appear in Annabelle's blue eyes. She could see a sermon rearing its ugly head and resented the fact she was about to be lectured like a child. She was a woman of seventeen years, after all!

Nonetheless, there was little she could do but meekly follow her hostess to the morning room.

'Sit down, Miss Annabelle,' said the Duchess with her chilly smile. 'I find it necessary to remind you that the Allsbury name is a very old one.'

'Yes,' said Annabelle, feeling younger by the minute.

'Our families are shortly to be allied,' went on her grace, 'and it is important to remember that conduct which would pass unnoticed in a country vicarage may not be becoming to an Allsbury.'

'You do my parents an injustice,' said Annabelle hotly. 'My father is very strict!'

'Indeed! From your conduct and speech last night, I assumed he was as I had heard him to be, a disciplined man on the hunting field and quite undisciplined off it.'

'If behaving like an Allsbury means criticizing your guests' parents, then I would rather not behave like an Allsbury,' said Annabelle, assuming a quaint dignity. 'By all means tell my father when you see him what you think of his character, your grace, but do not put me in the unfortunate position of defending a gentleman who needs no defence whatsoever.'

'Very well,' said the Duchess. 'Instead of telling *you* what I think of your language and manners, I shall write and tell your father.'

Annabelle went quite white and the Duchess surveyed

her with malicious satisfaction. Her grace had noticed the way Brabington's eyes rested too frequently on this pert miss, and she did not want such a matrimonial prize snatched away when she had young relatives resident who were more deserving of such a distinguished marriage. Also, if she riled the Reverend Charles Armitage in just the right way by criticizing Miss Annabelle, then he might forbid Minerva to marry Sylvester.

As if she had read her thoughts Annabelle said evenly, 'If you think that by complaining of me to papa will somehow cause a family row in which Minerva will be forbidden to marry your son, then I take leave to tell you, ma'am, that you do not know your son very well.'

'I made a mistake even in trying to talk to you,' said the Duchess haughtily. 'Your father will hear from me. Since you are here at my son's suggestion then I cannot unfortunately send you away, much as I would like to do so.'

'Good day to you, your grace,' said Annabelle with what the Duchess thought was a quite infuriating air of dignity.

Annabelle survived with her dignity intact until she reached the security of her bedroom where she flung herself face down on the bed and burst into tears. After a hearty bout of crying, she felt much better and all her old anger returned. Now more than ever was she determined to marry the Marquess.

If Annabelle had told Minerva of what the Duchess had said, then Minerva would have told Lord Sylvester, and there would have been no question of her grace writing to the vicar. But Annabelle was very jealous of Minerva and could only be glad that she had removed all traces of her weeping by the time Minerva softly entered the room and asked what the Duchess had said.

'Oh, it was nothing of any account,' said Annabelle airily. 'She thinks I am a child and should be constantly engaged in useful work. She wanted my assistance in completing some needlepoint for a firescreen and I said I would help her, but not today.

50

'I pleaded the headache. And you know, Merva, it is quite dreadful, for no sooner had I got here than I *did* begin to feel my head aching. Do make my excuses to Lady Coombes. If I lie down for a little, then I will feel quite the thing.'

'Of course,' said Minerva warmly. 'I am so relieved her grace said nothing to upset you. Sylvester feared she might, and sent me to find out. If she had lectured you too strongly, then he was going to deal with her himself. But I shall tell him there was nothing amiss and the Duchess only wished to give you some employ.'

Minerva's voice ended on a faint question as if she were not quite reassured.

'Oh, don't bother discussing me with your fiancé,' yawned Annabelle, stretching her arms. 'I am monstrous tired, Merva. Please leave me.'

'Very well,' said Minerva doubtfully. 'Do you wish me to come back in an hour to see if you need anything?'

'Don't fuss so!' snapped Annabelle, and then added in a milder tone, 'Only see how my poor aching head makes me tetchy. I will be all right if I am left alone.'

'Well, at least let me send one of the maids up with a hot posset.'

'*No.* Nothing will serve but peace and quiet.'

Minerva nodded doubtfully and went out and quietly closed the door.

'Thank goodness she has gone,' Annabelle told her reflection in the looking glass. 'Now, to paint, or not to paint.' Whether to renew the maquillage which had been washed away by her tears. Would he hold her in his arms today, after so short an acquaintance? If he did so, he might get paint on his coat.

She compromised by rubbing her cheeks to bring a high colour into them and then rang the bell for Betty.

When the maid arrived she said, 'Go and discreetly find out the whereabouts of the Marquess of Brabington, Betty. I have some intelligence from my father to impart.'

'Vicar'd tell Miss Minerva if he wished anything to be passed on,' said Betty suspiciously.

Annabelle swung around on her seat at the toilet table, her eyes blazing. 'How would you like to be whipped, Betty?' she screamed.

'I'd tell vicar if you did,' said Betty stoutly.

'Do as I tell you,' shouted Annabelle, 'or I shall pinch you and *pinch* you until you are black and blue.'

Betty could see Miss Bella working herself up into a tremendous passion and so she said a hurried 'Yes, miss,' and ducked out of the room quickly before Annabelle could throw anything at her.

She seemed to be away a very long time and Annabelle marched impatiently up and down the room, wondering if the maid had dared to defy her.

Just when she was about to ring the bell again, Betty returned, bearing a cup of herb tea. 'I'm sorry I was so long, miss,' she said, 'but Miss Minerva told me to bring you this and I had to go to the kitchens and wait until cook brewed it.'

'And?' queried Annabelle, a dangerous glint in her eye.

'And his lordship is in the library.'

'Thank you, Betty,' cooed Annabelle. 'You may put that disgusting concoction on the table and go. Wait a minute! You didn't tell Minerva I was looking for Lord Brabington?'

'No, miss,' said Betty, eyeing her suspiciously.

'Then don't, or it will be the worse for you. Don't stand there fidgeting and staring. Go!'

Annabelle took the cup of herb tea, tugged open the window and threw it out into the snow. Then she studied her reflection carefully in the looking glass, squared her shoulders and set off to capture the heart of the Marquess of Brabington.

It was a pity he was in the library, thought Annabelle, with a sudden stab of pain. That room seemed unlucky, somehow.

The Marquess was sitting in a winged chair by the fireplace, reading a book. The white glare from the snow outside made his pale face seem even whiter. He did not look up as Annabelle quietly entered, and she studied him for a few seconds before going forwards.

He had none of his friend Lord Sylvester's studied elegance. He exuded a powerful aura of virility and his hands holding the book were strong and square, unlike Lord Sylvester's very white, long-fingered ones.

Neither had he any of his lordship's cool, mocking mannerisms which made Annabelle's heart beat so fast. Although Annabelle had seen her sister clasped in Lord Sylvester's passionate embrace, she had shut that scene from her mind as much as possible. It was the perfection of Lord Sylvester's dress and his seeming absence of sexuality which attracted her so forcibly. But Annabelle did not know this. She considered herself the hot-blooded passionate one and Minerva the cool, aloof spinster, not knowing that deep in her maidenly soul she, Annabelle, was, in fact, very prudish. Although she had responded to Guy Wentwater's embraces, she did not realize her ardour was the result of triumph at having caught a beau so young. Also, she liked to think of herself as being superior to Minerva in every way, and so did not suspect that if Lord Sylvester had treated her to one iota of the passion which he bestowed on Minerva, then she would immediately have recoiled in horror. It would be as if a very beautiful and much admired statue had suddenly sprung to life and started sweating and panting.

She gave a little cough and the Marquess immediately lowered his book.

'Why, Miss Annabelle!' he exclaimed, struggling to his feet and clutching the chair-back for support.

'Please be seated, my lord,' said Annabelle. 'You are not well.'

He sank back down into the chair and gave her a rueful grin. 'I confess I am as weak as a kitten. What brings you here?'

'I came to see you, my lord,' said Annabelle softly. 'I thought I might read to you.'

'I have not lost the faculty of sight,' he said, looking amused. 'Which is just as well or I could not appreciate the beautiful vision you present.'

53

'Thank you, my lord,' Annabelle curtseyed demurely.

'Nonetheless,' he smiled, 'it would afford me a great deal of pleasure to hear your voice, and I confess to a feeling of wanting to be spoiled by a pretty girl.'

Annabelle pulled forwards a chair and sat next to him and held out her hand for the book.

'Letters!' said Annabelle, who had been hoping for a novel.

'I find them very interesting,' said the Marquess. 'They are written by a Mr Edward Burt who was General Wade's agent in the last century. He describes the Highlands of Scotland very well. I have never been as far north as the mountains of Scotland, and I am fascinated by his travels.'

Annabelle resigned herself. 'Where shall I begin?' she asked.

'Just there. Letter XXII. Where it begins, "The common habit".'

He settled back in his chair and Annabelle began to read. ' *"The common habit of the ordinary Highlanders is far from being acceptable to the eye; with them a small part of the plaid is set in folds and girt round the waist to make of it a short petticoat that reaches half way down the thigh, and the rest is brought over the shoulders, and then fastened before, below the neck, often with a fork, and sometimes with a bodkin, or sharpened piece of stick, so that they make pretty near the appearance of the poor women in London when they bring their gowns over their heads to shelter them from the rain.*

' *"In this way of wearing the plaid, they have sometimes nothing else to cover them, and are often barefoot; but some I have seen shod with a kind of pumps made out of a raw cowhide with the hair turned outward, which being ill made, the wearer's feet looked something like those of a rough-footed hen or pigeon; these are called* quarrants, *and are not only offensive to the sight, but intolerable to the smell of those who are near them. The stocking rises no higher than the thick of the calf, and from the middle of the thigh to the middle of the leg is a naked space, which being exposed to all weathers, becomes tanned and freckled; and the joint being mostly infected with the country distemper, the whole is very disagreeable to*

54

the eye.

' *"This dress is called the* quelt; *and for the most part they wear the petticoat so very short, that in a windy day, going up a hill, or stooping, the indecency of it is plainly discovered.*

' *"A Highland gentleman told me one day merrily, as we were speaking of a dangerous precipice we had passed over together, that a lady of noble family had complained to him very seriously, that as she was going over the same place with a* gilly, *who was upon an upper path leading her horse with a long string, she was so terrified with the sight of the abyss, that, to avoid it, she was forced to look up towards the bare Highlander all the way long".'*

Annabelle giggled and the Marquess looked up with a start and held out his hand for the book.

'I beg your pardon, Miss Annabelle,' he said. 'I was so engrossed with the sound of your bewitching voice that I had forgot the subject matter might not be suitable for the eyes of a *lady.*'

'Is he describing the *kilt?*' asked Annabelle, who was in fact rather relieved to find some fact could be as entertaining as fiction.

'I believe so. He spells the word phonetically. *Quelt* means kilt.'

'I am so disappointed,' mourned Annabelle. 'From the poems of Mr Walter Scott I had formed a more romantic picture of the Highlander.'

'Some of the chiefs and lords I met in Edinburgh look very fine in their national dress. This describes the dress of the poor Highlander, and I gather from friends that the poverty in the North is still appalling.'

He spoke seriously and Annabelle dropped her eyelashes to mask her expression of total indifference. The Highlands of Scotland and their inhabitants seemed to her as remote as the West Indies.

'But,' went on the Marquess in a rallying tone, 'if the gossips in this house have it aright, it was *you* who seemed to have a charming capacity for putting the company to the blush.'

'I *did* use some terrible cant,' said Annabelle with a charming air of candour. 'But in truth I did not know

55

what I said. I thought it was fashionable to use cant.'

'Not in ladies and not in mixed company for *anyone.*'

'I should have known better,' sighed Annabelle, ''than to listen to a couple of back gammon players.'

'My *dear* Miss Annabelle!'

'Oh, dear, what have I said now?'

'I could not possibly explain.'

'But it was a very respectable coachman who said that. He said, ''Them back gammon players makes me want to flash my hash.''''

'Worse and worse,' said the Marquess, burying his head in his hands.

'Now, you must tell me or I shall ask Minerva.'

'Do. She will not know – fortunately – what you are talking about.'

'But *she* will ask Lord Sylvester.'

'Very well. It is either my blushes or Sylvester's, and I am informed that my face lacks colour. I will translate.

'Back gammon players are gentleman who prefer the company of their own sex.'

'As do most men,' said Annabelle, surprised. 'Else why do you all congregate in coffee houses and clubs?'

'That is as far as I am prepared to go. To flash your hash means to vomit.'

'Well, *that* is not so bad. What does old hat mean?' said Annabelle provocatively, as if she did not know – now – what it meant.

'Miss Annabelle, if you persist in sullying that pretty mouth of yours with disgusting language, I shall be tempted to kiss it clean.'

Annabelle raised her fan to make one of the many gestures with which a lady received an overwarm remark from a gentleman. She could rap him playfully on the wrist or raise the fan to cover her blushes.

Instead, she stopped with the fan half-raised and looked at him with wide blue eyes.

'Then why don't you?' she said.

'Brazen hussy!'

'Ah, you were funning. And I heard you called a very

brave man.'

He leaned forwards and took her chin gently in his hand. Annabelle closed her eyes. The Marquess kissed her gently on the mouth and then drew away murmuring, 'I thought Sylvester held your affections.'

'He is engaged to my sister, sir!'

'Ah.'

'Is it you, my lord, who ... who ... I have formed a *tendre* for you, my lord.'

'You are so very young, Annabelle.'

'It seems the Armitage girls are destined to fall in love with men in their dotage.'

He looked deep into her eyes. Annabelle conjured up Lord Sylvester's face, imagined it was he who was gazing into her eyes, and her own glowed with warmth and love.

The Marquess took a deep breath and said half to himself, 'I would be a fool to let such a moment go by.'

He took her hand in his. 'Annabelle,' he said. 'We hardly know each other, and, yes, your youth is a great disadvantage. No. Let me speak. The man you will want at twenty-one may not be the man you want now. We shall get to know each other, first as friends, and then, if I am convinced that your mind is set, I shall write to your father and ask his permission to pay my addresses.'

A heady feeling of triumph assailed Annabelle. She had won! Now all she had to do was to play her cards aright and soon she would be able to plead prettily that she be married at the same time as Minerva.

He rested his head against the wing of the chair, his face suddenly white and drawn.

'Leave me now, my child,' he said faintly. 'I am curst weak.'

Annabelle stood up. 'I shall send help,' she said anxiously.

'Simply ring that bell over there and I shall do the rest,' he said. 'Go now. I shall see you again soon.'

Annabelle rang the bell and then hurried from the room. She would not tell Minerva or anyone until it was a *fait accompli*. Now she would need to bribe Betty with a scarf or some trinket to make sure that upstart miss kept her mouth firmly shut.

After she had left, the Marquess of Brabington was helped by two stout footmen to his bedchamber. He lay back against the pillows staring up at the canopy, his hands behind his head. What did he *really* know of Miss Annabelle? Had he been too precipitate? But somehow he found he could not think beyond her beauty. He had been dazzled from the first moment he had set eyes on her. Then her memory had faded a little. He was always conscious of the difference in their ages.

But he loved her, he thought with a smile. And that was too rare and beautiful a thing to be picked over and analysed. He closed his eyes and settled down for sleep, seeing his life stretching out in front of him, one long, sunny road with Annabelle on his arm; a laughing, enchanting, adoring Annabelle, forever beautiful, forever happy, and quite, quite uncomplicated.

The following days were to be passed without a glimpse of the Marquess. It was said he had a high fever and Annabelle fretted as the physician came and went. Lord Sylvester always seemed to be watching her curiously, and she had to endure the fact that her love for him had not abated one whit.

At last came the glad news that the Marquess's fever had abated and that he was recovering quickly. The ladies of the house, with the exception of the Duchess, had quite warmed to Annabelle since she now appeared quiet and reserved, seeming to take no interest in the gentlemen whatsoever.

And then after a thaw and a following driving wind, the Reverend Charles Armitage, vicar of St Charles and St Jude, made his arrival.

Annabelle heard his loud voice as she was descending the stairs and peeped over the bannisters.

The vicar was standing in the hall, clutching a letter in one hand, his face grim. Before him stood the Duchess of Allsbury.

'What's this here,' the vicar was demanding, 'about

Bella behaving bad?'

'I think she should answer for herself,' said the Duchess coolly. 'Her behaviour has been quite pretty of late but one shudders to think of a recurrence of her disgraceful manners.'

Annabelle heard a step behind her and swung around to find the Marquess of Brabington smiling down at her.

Down below in the hall, the angry vicar had been joined by Minerva and Lord Sylvester. Annabelle shuddered before the wrath of her father to come; like a child, she turned and pressed her face into the Marquess's coat and whispered, 'I'm afraid. Papa will horsewhip me.'

The Marquess put an arm about her and held her close. He knew his worth on the marriage market. He knew the one way to allay any parent's wrath was to present himself as a future son-in-law. And yet ... and yet ... it was a great step to take.

He raised her face and looked down into her eyes. 'If he knew we were to be married, he would no longer be angry,' he murmured half to himself.

Annabelle's beautiful blue eyes blazed with hope as she put up her hands and clung to his lapels.

'Do you love me?' he asked softly.

'Yes,' gasped Annabelle desperately. 'Oh, *yes.*'

'Then let us greet your father,' he said, tucking her arm in his.

All faces turned up to them as they descended the stairs.

'See here, Bella ...' began the vicar.

'Ah, Mr Armitage,' said the Marquess smoothly. 'You are arrived just in time. It is rather a public place to ask you for your permission to pay my addresses to your daughter, Annabelle, but that is what I wish to do.'

'*What!*' Anger was chased away by amazement to be replaced by a look of joy. His Bella to marry a marquess. The vicar dropped the Duchess's letter on the floor, held out his arms and Annabelle rushed into them.

'Hey, my pretty puss,' said the vicar, rumpling her bright curls. 'Couldn't wait for a Season before you got wed?'

He released her and went to shake hands with the Marquess. 'Of course, you have my blessing,' he said, striking that young man jovially on the shoulder. 'I thought I had made a mistake letting you go, Bella, but I cry *peccavi*.'

'And there is more marvellous news,' said Annabelle, smiling at Minerva. 'Peter has agreed that we shall have a *double* wedding. I will be married in the same church and at the same time as my dear sister!'

Lord Sylvester noticed a strange, rather quizzical expression crossing the Marquess's face.

But Minerva rushed forwards, her face radiant, and enfolded her sister in a warm embrace.

'I am *so* happy Annabelle,' she said with tears in her eyes.

Annabelle drew back a little and frowned. 'You are not mad at me, Merva, for arranging to share your wedding?'

'*Mad*? Of *course* not. It is the most wonderful thing. Now my wedding day will be doubly blessed!' said Minerva, clasping her hands as if she were praying.

Hearing the commotion, the rest of the guests crowded into the hall to find out what was going on.

Annabelle was soon surrounded by a sort of bewilderment of congratulations. Her heart hammered as a voice nagged over and over in her brain, 'Minerva did not mind *at all*. I have not scored one hit. And I am affianced to one man and – God help me – in love with t'other!'

CHAPTER FOUR

Perhaps if the Marquess of Brabington had not been so ill, he would have managed to see more of his fiancée before her departure to Hopeworth.

As it was, it was only after Annabelle had left that the Marquess realized they had never been alone together. Such moments as they had had were usually spent in one of the many rooms of the Abbey while the rest of the guests sat around.

He had taxed her on her wish to be married at the same time as her sister, but Annabelle had only fixed him with an innocent blue stare and had said, 'Peter, I *told* you, I'm sure I did. It is certainly very rushed. Do you want to wait?'

And the Marquess, of course, did not want to wait. He was very much in love, so much in love that he forebore from pointing out that she had no time to tell him about wedding arrangements during a ten-second proposal.

His illness had robbed him of much of his commonsense and humour, and so he was out of balance. He had been in love before, at a time when he had neither title nor money. The lady had encouraged his affections only to turn him down in favour of an elderly lord. He had acquired his title and fortune a week before her wedding, and had been appalled when she had called at his house, saying that she had always loved him, and begging him to rescue her from a loveless marriage. Her motives were dreadfully plain. Since then, he had thrown himself into his army career, viewing society women from then on with a certain detached amusement.

But Annabelle had caught him at a weak moment. Certainly he had been enchanted with her from the first time he set eyes on her, but, in normal circumstances, his natural prudence would have told him not to rush into too

61

hasty a marriage.

He was also much influenced by the fact that his friend, Lord Sylvester, was to marry into the same family. He trusted Sylvester's cool judgement and never paused to think that two very different birds could come from the same family nest.

He was tired of wars and adventures and was anxious to settle down. He was prepared to resign himself to a round of London amusements first, since he considered it would be unfair to deprive his young bride of all the pleasures he had himself begun to find wearisome.

Lord Sylvester, after lazily offering his congratulations, had spoken no more on the subject of his friend's marriage and the Marquess took his subsequent silence for approval. He would have been amazed had he known that Lord Sylvester was extremely worried.

In Minerva's case, commonsense had been overridden by family loyalty, and she assured Lord Sylvester that Annabelle was deeply in love with the Marquess.

Lord Sylvester was anxious to believe Minerva. But there was one thing he could not bring himself to tell her.

He had been all too well aware of Annabelle's infatuation for him. And although he had thought it quickly over, he could not rid himself of the impression that she was jealous of Minerva and was marrying Peter simply in a spirit of sisterly rivalry.

The Marquess had planned to leave Haeter Abbey at the same time as Annabelle, but he had been summoned to Horseguards to give evidence in an enquiry into the sufficiency, or insufficiency, of army rations, and was too much of a soldier to beg liberty for personal reasons.

Lord Sylvester was anxious to return to his own estates to deal with matters there, since he had promised his bride a travelling honeymoon through such countries as were left free of Napoleon's rule.

Annabelle had become accustomed to life at the Abbey. It was like living in a very grandly equipped village, she thought. She had explored everywhere, from the rich state apartments inside to the granary, dairies, stables, pottery, carpenter's shop, gardens, succession houses, and deer park on the outside. The vicarage loomed very dark, small and poky in her memory. But Minerva had received a letter from Mrs Armitage who complained bitterly about her failing health brought about by the onerous duties of the parish.

Deirdre and Daphne were in trouble. They had dressed Farmer Baxter's prize pig in one of Frederica's gowns and had driven it across the village green. This had fortunately happened when the vicar was at the Abbey and his wrath had not been quite what it might had he been present at the time.

Now the vicar was home and it was time for the girls to return as well. Annabelle had begged Minerva to extend their stay, but Minerva had pointed out that the Duchess would not appreciate their presence a day longer, and for her part, she did not want to stay on when her fiancé was planning to leave.

And so the two sisters set out for home on a bitterly cold day. The snow which had fallen on the day that Annabelle had talked to the Marquess in the library had thawed and frozen and thawed and frozen so that the roads were full of treacherous, hard ruts. The maid, Betty, had contracted a severe cold and was to follow later.

The wedding was to be held in St George's, Hanover Square, in London, with full pomp and circumstance. Annabelle knew that the Duchess could hardly be expected to furnish a wedding dress for *her* and was fretting over the idea that she would be outshone by Minerva who would be wearing several thousands of guineas' worth of Brussels lace.

As the carriage jolted along, she cast a sideways glance at her sister's pensive face. 'Glad to be going home, Merva?' she asked.

'Yes, particularly as Sylvester is leaving as well,' said Minerva calmly. 'It will not be long until we are both married, Bella. I wish it were not going to be such a grand wedding. I wanted to be married by papa in the church at home, but her grace insisted on a big London wedding, and Sylvester pointed out that it does not matter where we are married so long as we *are* married.'

'Church weddings are not at all fashionable,' sniffed Annabelle. 'We could both have been married at the Abbey.'

'We could hardly do that when father is a minister of God,' pointed out Minerva.

'Oh, it's easy for you to be so calm about it all,' snapped Annabelle. 'You will be very fine in that grand gown the Duchess is giving you. What am I to wear? Something from the village dressmaker?'

'But I thought Peter would have told you ...' began Minerva.

'Lord Brabington to you,' said Annabelle in order to get revenge for the time Minerva had corrected *her* when she had called Lord Sylvester Comfrey, 'Sylvester'.

'As I was saying,' said Minerva severely, 'I am amazed Lord Brabington did not explain to you how matters stood. I had discussed the wedding arrangements with him and explained my own gown was to be very fine, and I was worried about providing you with something which would at least look as good. He promptly said he would write to Madame Verné in London – she is the *best* dressmaker you know – and ask her to send sketches to Hopeworth. We are to travel to London, a month before the wedding, and stay with Lady Godolphin so that your gown may be made very quickly.'

'I am not a child!' exclaimed Annabelle. 'Why were such arrangements made behind my back? And I have hardly had any occasion to speak to my fiancé in private since we announced our engagement,' she added, her voice beginning to rise with temper, forgetting that she had carefully avoided being alone with the Marquess. 'How did *you* come to be so intimate with him!'

'I merely went to see him to discuss the arrangements.'

'Where? Where did this discussion take place?'

'In his bedchamber.'

'WHAT!'

'Annabelle, do not be so missish. I am the eldest of the

family and you know I have long been accustomed to organizing things for us. It was natural I should go to see Lord Brabington. Since he was convalescing, I could not very well have an audience with him anywhere else.'

'I,' said Annabelle passionately, 'was *warned* by that *bat* of a Duchess that I must not go *near* Peter's room because it was not *comme il faut* – or comma fault as that stupid, gross travesty of a woman, Lady Godolphin, called it ...'

'That is quite enough,' interrupted Minerva in glacial tones.

'Don't come Miss Prunes and Prisms with *me!*' howled Annabelle. 'I, at least, can *wait* till my wedding night.'

The old Minerva would have blushed from the soles of her feet to the top of her head, but the new Minerva had an uncomfortably shrewd look in her eye.

'And what gave you the idea, miss, that I was beforehand in my behaviour?'

'One has only got to look at you,' said Annabelle sulkily.

'I am surprised that you have so much time to worry about my morals,' said Minerva. 'Look at me, Annabelle! Are you in love with Lord Brabington?'

'Of course I am, you widgeon. I'm marrying him, aren't I?'

'Yes,' said Minerva, half to herself. 'But if you are so very much in love, then why is your wedding gown so important to you?'

'Having already got a very beautiful one yourself, you can have a mind above such petty matters,' sneered Annabelle.

'I have, perhaps, become too accustomed to speak to you as if you were a child,' said Minerva slowly. 'I do worry about you, Annabelle. Mama's frequent illness, imagined or no, had put certain responsibilities on me. I still look on you as a child in my charge. Seventeen is not so very old after all.'

'Old enough to resent your perpetual lecturing and moralizing.'

'Do I?' said Minerva sadly. 'I suppose I do. Sylvester

tells me I am the real preacher of the Armitage family.'

'Does he, indeed,' said Annabelle, brightening. 'Tell me, Minerva, do many of the fashionable ladies have affairs?'

'I am afraid they do,' said Minerva in a low voice. 'You should see them, Bella. They are poor things; restless, hungry. It is as well for us that we shall never have to contemplate such a life. Why on earth did you ask such a question?'

'Because,' said Annabelle, leaning across the carriage and giving her sister a warm hug, 'I wanted to change the conversation. I am such a bear and you must forgive me. I am frightened of all the fuss, Merva, and that is what makes me such a crosspatch.'

'Oh, Bella, so am I,' said Minerva with relief as she hugged her sister back. 'Never mind, at least we shall be together.'

Annabelle settled back in her corner of the carriage, her thoughts busy. Lord Sylvester would soon tire of Minerva. And perhaps he would be glad to flirt a little with such a delicious young matron as the new Marchioness of Brabington. Almost she could hear him saying, 'You bore me, Minerva. I wish I had married your sister instead!'

She was just settling down to enjoy this rosy fantasy when she realized with irritation that Minerva was speaking again.

'And you should not be so harsh about Lady Godolphin,' Minerva was saying. 'It is extremely kind of her to invite us to London.'

'And who is footing the bill, pray?'

'Well, as a matter of fact, Sylvester said he would pay her for any expense incurred on our behalf, but she does not *need* to invite us.'

Annabelle sniffed. 'I suppose she can be amusing. She is a sort of walking parlour game. It became quite fun seeing which one of us could guess what she meant by one of her terrible Malapropisms. But no one guessed the last one. What did she mean when she said that the portrait at the end of the Long Gallery, just above the Meissen figures, was "catter chintzy"? No one could guess and Mr Frampton was offering a prize of five guineas to anyone who found the right answer.'

Minerva smiled. 'My lady meant *quattrocento*. Lord Sylvester was the winner.'

'Well, I was glad papa did not stay overlong. He was making quite a cake of himself over Lady Godolphin. Colonel Brian was not amused.'

'Papa was merely being gallant,' said Minerva. 'I do wish Colonel Brian and Lady Godolphin would legalize their arrangement.'

'Legalize? You mean *marry*? You mean he ... she ... oh, tish, Minerva. They are too old.'

'It seems some of us never outgrow our passions,' sighed Minerva. 'But what worries me is ... you must promise not to tell a soul, Bella, not even Peter.'

'I promise,' said Annabelle eagerly, delighted to find her prim sister was not above gossip.

'It is all very scandalous, you see, but rather sad in a way, for Colonel Brian was married and his wife was an invalid. But Lady Godolphin does not expect Colonel Brian to propose marriage because ... because she does not know his wife died last summer. Of course, he should observe at least a year's mourning, but Sylvester tells me Lady Godolphin has been kept in ignorance of Mrs Brian's death, the Colonel going so far as to keep the intelligence of it from the newspapers.'

'Dear, dear,' said Annabelle, her blue eyes sparkling. 'Wouldn't the fur and feathers fly if she ever found out!'

'Lady Godolphin will not find out unless the Colonel himself tells her.

'Sylvester came upon the truth of the matter by accident. *He* would never dream of telling her anything so cruel, nor would I, and you certainly must not. Don't look so ... *malicious*, Annabelle. I wish I had not told you.'

'I? I have no interest in what she does,' shrugged Annabelle. 'At her age, it is disgusting.'

Minerva looked at her sister but did not reply. Annabelle fell back into her fantasy of luring Lord Sylvester away from Minerva, and Minerva fought down strange new feelings that were welling up inside her. She was appalled to find that she was almost beginning to *dislike* Annabelle.

The thought was so painful, so treacherous, that she immediately fought it down and turned her attention to the passing countryside.

After a long and weary journey, they arrived at the vicarage. Annabelle did not even stay to put off her bonnet but immediately ran off to the Hall to tell her triumph to Josephine and Emily.

Minerva was surrounded by her younger sisters. She answered their questions automatically, looking through the vicarage window at Annabelle's flying figure, a little crease of worry between her brows.

Mrs Armitage trailed languidly in, a chiffon scarf drooping from one hand, and a limp ostrich feather fan from one wrist. She was a short, slightly plump woman, so there was not really enough of her to supply a dramatic droop. She only succeeded in looking rather round-shouldered. Minerva listened patiently while Mrs Armitage went on at length about all the gamut of emotions she had run on hearing the news of Annabelle's success.

At last, the vicar cut her short by jerking his head in the direction of his study and saying impatiently, 'Come along, Minerva.'

Minerva went reluctantly. She hoped she was not going to be asked for her views on Annabelle's engagement.

She began to relax as the vicar made no mention of it. He discussed arrangements for the wedding. Minerva and Annabelle were to go alone, Mrs Armitage feeling she could not endure a whole month in London, and even the lure of London chemists and London physicians was not enough to encourage her to face the prospect.

The rest of the family were to arrive a week before the wedding.

'Got quite a shock when I saw Lady Godolphin,' said the vicar meditatively. 'Quite a belle she was in her day. Still, she's lost none of her old charm, quite fascinating in a wrinkled and flabby kind of way.'

He pulled himself together with a jerk, flushed slightly, and said, 'Is that colonel her lover?'

'My dear papa,' lied Minerva. 'I do not know.'

'I suppose he is. She told me she had become quite demin-mundane and was living a life of oddity. I assume she meant adultery.'

'Perhaps she really meant oddity,' suggested Minerva, anxious not to be drawn on the subject. 'She often uses the right word.'

'Perhaps. Well, off with you, miss. There's still work to be done around here. Brabington has been very generous in the matter of the marriage settlement, and he don't want no dowry, so it looks as if we can hire some sort o' governess for the gels.'

'That would be wonderful,' said Minerva. 'Deirdre is still too young and a trifle wild to take over my duties.'

She kissed him on the cheek and turned to go.

'Minerva!'

Minerva turned round. The vicar had risen and was standing with his back to the fire, his coat tails hitched up over his bottom. 'Don't worry about Bella,' he said.

'I am very happy for her.'

'No, you ain't. You're worried sick because you feel sure she's marrying Brabington just because she wants to be a marchioness. And you're right. She's got another worse reason for doin' it in that cockloft o' hers. But it'll all work out in the end. Brabington'll school her, you'll see.'

'But I don't want him to *have* to school her,' said Minerva. 'I want it to be a love match.'

'Well, them sort o' marriages is deuced rare. Women are not all as lucky as you, my puss.'

'What is the other reason?' asked Minerva.

'Tell you some day,' said the vicar. 'Off with you!'

But as Minerva softly closed the door behind her, she thought she heard him mutter, 'Hope you don't find out first.'

Annabelle returned from the Hall in a pensive mood. Of course, Josephine and Emily had been wildly jealous. She had not expected anything else. But they had concealed it in an admirable way. They had affected kindness, they had affected deep concern over poor little Annabelle's rustic manners and dress and had told her terrible stories about ladies who were forced to rusticate in the country forever because they had done something quite awful like crossing their legs in public. Annabelle had quickly uncrossed hers.

Was she never to achieve one little bit of the triumphs she had dreamed of?

But there was the wedding. All society would be there. All London – that was the London bounded by St James's Square and Grosvenor Square – would be watching her. Annabelle's mind refused to take in the realities of marriage and what lay after the wedding. That was a vague and pleasant world of balls and parties with a complaisant Marquess somewhere in the background, someone to take her there and bring her back while she danced with Lord Sylvester.

It was balm to her soul to find a very respectful Deirdre waiting for her. Annabelle sat down at the toilet table and unpinned her bonnet while Deirdre sat on the bed behind her.

'It is a very fine thing to be marrying a marquess,' said Deirdre with a flattering tinge of awe in her voice. 'You know, I s'pose you really *are* quite pretty, Annabelle.'

'Beautiful is the word,' laughed Annabelle. 'And Madame Verné is to make my bride gown, Deirdre; she is the best in London. I think I shall have a very long train and the twins can be my pages. A little seed pearl embroidery, I think. I wonder whether the Prince Regent will come.'

'Tell me about it,' urged Deirdre, sitting in a half crouch.

'I am, amn't I?' said Annabelle crossly. 'Did the sketches arrive yet from Madame Verné? Oh, and will she be making the bridesmaids' gowns as well? Pink would be pretty. But you have got such an unfortunate colour of hair that pink would not suit *at all.*'

'That's not what I wanted to hear,' said Deirdre scornfully. 'I want to hear about *love.*'

'Oh, that,' said Annabelle carelessly, patting her blonde curls. 'You are too young.'

'Not I. Perhaps it is you who are too young, Bella. You are like a child with a glittering toy. What will you do with your Marquess once the novelty has worn off? You can't very well put him away in the attic.'

'Get out of here!' screamed Annabelle, in sudden rage. 'Out! Out! *Out!*'

Deirdre stuck out her tongue and scampered to the door.

Annabelle sat breathing heavily for a few moments after she had left. She felt a sudden stab of unease, and then shrugged. The Marquess had said nothing about selling his commission. The war was still going on. With any luck he would soon be back on the high sierras of Spain.

The few weeks before their departure to London were exhausting. The parish rounds had to be performed as if the two girls were not just about to marry into the nobility. Bundles of blankets and food had to be collected for the poor and distributed at the parish hall. The poor had to be visited, cordials and medicine and calves' foot jelly carried in a heavy basket.

Lady Wentwater had gone off on some mysterious visit so at least she didn't have to be read to.

Sketches had arrived, not only for the bride's gown but for the bridesmaids' dresses. Annabelle had gone into *alt,* demanding that the girls would wear what she chose.

The vicar put an end to the row by gathering up the

precious sketches and departing with them to his study. To Annabelle's horror, she found out that he had chosen the gowns himself and had sent them off post-haste to London. To all her rage, he had merely replied calmly that if she persisted in behaving like a child, then she would be treated like one.

He then punished her by making her exercise his hounds, adding that he had a good mind to give her a beating instead.

Annabelle felt very ill-used. The budding conscience about tricking the Marquess which was beginning to nag her was quickly nipped by her fury at her father's treatment of her. Now more than ever did she wish to be married and become her own mistress.

The Marquess's face grew fainter in her mind, and soon she dreamt only of Lord Sylvester, perpetual dreamlike ballrooms sailing through her head, endless routs and parties where they would exchange passionate, meaningful looks across the room.

It was a blustery day at the end of February when she and Minerva at last set out. A great roaring wind was whipping the branches of the trees and tearing the clouds to rags. The village pond had turned into a miniature Atlantic and one of the tall chimneys of the Hall had fallen through the roof of the East Wing, injuring no one and causing the vicar a deal of quiet satisfaction, since his brother, Sir Edwin, had been pontificating only the week before about how he could not supply money to repair the roof of the church and pointing out how *he* always kept his property in order.

The two sisters were very quiet. Minerva was sad at saying farewell to her little sisters. Annabelle was feeling uneasy. Now that she had left the vicarage, it seemed a warm refuge, and the prospect of the future a terrifying unknown.

A pale shaft of sunshine gilded the thatch of the cottages around the pond. Annabelle looked out at the village as if she would never see it again. Every stone, every blade of grass seemed sharply etched.

Out on the Hopeminster Road there were already signs of spring. Rooks were building nests in the tall trees which bordered the brown ploughed fields. The branches of the pussy willows were tipped with little white balls, like balls of cotton wool, and in the grass verges beside the road clumps of snowdrops shone whitely through melting patches of ice.

The wind roared across the fields and sang in the trees.

If only, thought Annabelle, I could stop the carriage, and open the door and run away across the fields before the wind, and never return until everyone had forgotten about this marriage of mine.

But reality soon crowded back. The shame of returning the presents, the explanations, and above all, Lord Sylvester would never forgive her for jilting his best friend.

The fact that Lord Sylvester, disenchanted with Minerva or not, would, by the same token, hardly enter into a liaison with his wife's sister and the wife of his best friend did not appear to trouble her thoughts.

Annabelle could not imagine the great love she held for Lord Sylvester never being reciprocated. And like most people deeply in love with the wrong person, she was convinced it was *right* somehow. All must be sacrified at the altar flame of this pure passion. Lesser mortals did not feel as she, nor were they capable of the same intensity of feeling.

In other words, Minerva wouldn't mind very much ...

CHAPTER FIVE

The Armitage sisters had been resident in London for some two weeks. Annabelle was shakily beginning to find her feet. The Marquess was at Portsmouth on military business, Lord Sylvester had not returned from the country, London was thin of company, but what she had so far met was terrifying enough.

She was quickly to find out that beauty without fortune, and beauty already engaged, was of little interest to the London *ton*. Her frequent attempts to attract the attention of the company to herself were frowned upon. It was irritating, too, to note that Minerva did not seem to suffer from the snubs she herself had to endure. Furthermore the Pinks of the Ton did not wish to listen to a young miss from the country with views of her own and Annabelle was quickly abandoned for some plain young girl who knew how to flirt with a fan and simper to a nicety.

Annabelle was unaware that during the height of the Season, she would be considered a reigning belle; that only the hardened bachelors who were more interested in their clothes than the ladies were to be found in the saloons of London at present.

Her vanity deserted her, and when the boys had leave from school, she cheerfully volunteered to cancel her social engagements so that she could take them to see the wild animals on 'Change and to Westminster Abbey and Astley's Amphitheatre.

Still very much of a schoolgirl, Annabelle enjoyed these unsophisticated delights to the hilt.

On her return to Lady Godolphin's mansion in Hanover Square she was informed by Mice, her ladyship's butler, that the Marquess of Brabington was awaiting her in the Green Saloon and that my lady and Miss Armitage were absent from the house.

74

Annabelle tripped lightly into the Green Saloon to find the Marquess standing in front of the fireplace. She had enjoyed her day, her vanity had been crushed with the lack of attention she had received in London, and these two factors combined to make her very glad to see the Marquess indeed.

She hugged him unaffectedly, her face glowing from the cold, and the Marquess felt all his worries ebb away. He had begun to have niggling doubts about the warmth of his love's affections. She had replied to none of his letters. But when he felt her arms go about him in the most natural way in the world, his heart leapt, and he kissed her lightly on the cheek, and led her to a sofa where he drew her down beside him.

'I have missed you,' he said warmly. 'Where have you been today?'

'Taking my two small brothers to see the sights,' said Annabelle. 'In truth I enjoyed it more than any of the grand balls or parties I have attended.'

This was very much to the Marquess's way of thinking. He took her hand in his and smiled down at her. 'I called on Sylvester on the way back and he sends his love.'

Annabelle's face shone with an almost religious radiance. He had sent his *love*. Ambition, vanity, love and longing came crowding back into her brain. Oh, if only this Marquess did not mean to sell out of the army.

'When may we expect Lord Sylvester back in Town?' asked Annabelle, wondering if she could draw her hand away without offending him.

'Tomorrow,' he said. He was about to go on to tell Annabelle how anxious Lord Sylvester was to see Minerva again, but Annabelle suddenly said, 'We have not discussed what you will do after we are married.'

'Why, I will be married to you, my sweeting.'

'I mean, will you be rejoining your regiment?'

The Marquess looked thoughtfully at the fire and gave a little sigh. 'I suppose my days of fighting are over,' he said. 'I would love to be in at the kill when we finally drive the French over the Pyrenees. But I will be a married man, and then, added to that, there are the responsibilities of my estates. I cannot remain an absentee landlord all my life.'

'The war cannot go on forever,' said Annabelle throwing her head back in a noble way that was reminiscent of the old Minerva. 'If you would rather fight for your country than stay with me, I will understand.'

He held her hand in a tighter clasp. 'You are an amazing girl, Annabelle. The war has many hardships, but ...'

He fell silent, remembering the rough sedge mats spread out under the trees at night, the accoutrements hanging from the branches, the bundle of fine branches to lie on and the green sod for a pillow. Remembering the screech from the bullock carts laden with the maggot-infested bodies of the dead or dying; remembering the mad exhilaration of battle and the comradeship of his men.

'But it is no place for a woman,' laughed Annabelle.

'Oh, there are women enough.'

'But *such* women!'

'No, I do not mean camp followers. I mean the wives – particularly the Irish wives. Incredible bravery and fortitude.

'There was a laundress called Biddy whose husband, Dan, was a soldier in the 34th. We were retreating last winter and the French were hard at our heels.

'Her husband was wounded and he dropped down by the roadside saying he could go no further. She told him to get on her back and she would carry him, but the man refused to part with either his knapsack or his firelock. She knew the French would be on them soon, and so, in desperation, she decided to carry the lot. I can still remember her Irish brogue. She said, "Well, sir, I went away wid him on me back, knapsack, firelock and all, as strong as Samson for the fear I was in, an' fegs, I carried him half a league after the regiment into the bivwack; an' me back was bruck entirely from that time to this, an' it'll never get strait till I go to the Holy Well in Ireland, and have Father McShane's blessin', an' his hands laid over me!" '

Annabelle eyed her beloved nervously. Was he hinting that *she* should follow the drum?

'There are no *ladies* who go to war!' she exclaimed.

'Well,' he laughed, 'women like that laundress are very great ladies in my opinion. But if you mean ladies of quality, yes, most certainly. The most famous beauty we have to lighten our days is the former Juanita Maria de los Dolores de Leon. After the capture of Bajadoz, two ladies, sisters, both of them Spanish, threw themselves on the mercy of the British. Juanita was fifteen and the most beautiful creature anyone had ever seen. Two days later she was married to Captain Harry Smith of the Rifles, and, since then, she has been the darling of the army, sharing all our adventures and hardships.'

Annabelle became more than ever convinced that he expected her to volunteer to join him. For a moment she indulged in a brief dream in which she became the heroine and darling of the British army herself, but then Lord Sylvester's face swam into her mind, and she set her lips in a stubborn line.

'I do not think mama's health could stand the shock if I were to go to war with you,' she said.

'I would not let you,' he laughed. 'You are not the stuff that heroines are made of. I mean, heroines of war,' he added hastily.

'Then you will rejoin your regiment?'

'Give me time,' he said slowly. 'No one expects me to rush back so soon after my wedding. Enough of this talk of war. You have not kissed me, my love.'

'Oh, we must not!' said Annabelle hastily. 'I am not chaperoned and Mice has left the door open, you see, and someone might come in or Minerva might return.'

'Annabelle, my love, I would swear you are afraid of me.'

Annabelle hung her head. 'Merely shy,' she whispered.

'Pre-wedding nerves,' he said sympathetically. He raised her hand and kissed it. 'I am prepared to wait till we are married. You will find me very patient.'

'Thank you,' said Annabelle, feling quite miserable with guilt. He looked so handsome, so *caring*, those strange eyes of his golden in the firelight.

'My parents are dead, as you know,' he said, releasing her hand and searching in one of his pockets. 'But these belong to the Marchionesses of Brabington.' He handed her a flat box.

Annabelle slowly opened it. An attractive and colourful antique necklace and brooch glittered and sparkled up at her in the light. It was made in the Renaissance style with a design of blue and white scrolls and crimson annular motifs, set with rubies, diamonds and baroque pearl drops.

'Come over to the looking-glass and see how it looks,' he urged.

Annabelle arose reluctantly. She handed him the box and stood like an obedient child while he fastened the jewels about her neck.

She stood very still, feeling the heavy weight of the necklace against her bosom. With the weight of the jewels came the terrible weight of the reality of marriage. In all her dreams of Lord Sylvester she had ignored, until now, the fact that Peter, Marquess of Brabington, was in love with her. And he was convinced she was in love with him.

Annabelle's better self, long dormant, rose to the surface. The wedding must be called off. Father would horsewhip her. There would never be any Season for her after the storm of shame had subsided. With luck, she might eventually marry some unassuming county gentleman.

'Well?' he said teasingly. 'You are very quiet.'

She swung around to face him.

'Peter,' she said, 'there is something I must tell you ...'

'Annabelle!' came a joyful cry from the hall. The drawing room door burst open and Minerva sailed in. 'Look who I found on the doorstep!'

Following her came Lord Sylvester Comfrey.

'Peter, my boy,' he said. 'You look fit. Well, here we all

are. All ready to meet at the altar.' He caught Minerva to him with an arm around her waist and she turned a laughing face up to him.

Jealousy, horrible, green-eyed, scaled and clawed, raged through Annabelle and she put a possessive hand on the Marquess's arm.

'See what Peter has given me? Aren't they superb?'

She laughed and pirouetted in front of them, while Minerva laughed as well to see her sister so happy and the Marquess looked on with an indulgent smile.

'I shall be the most pampered bride in London,' said Annabelle breathlessly. She stretched up and kissed the Marquess on the cheek. As she turned back, she caught a look of worry and pain in Lord Sylvester's green eyes – and then it was gone.

A heady feeling of triumph rose up in her. He *cared*. He was jealous. She would go through with this marriage, since both she and Sylvester were honour bound to keep their promises.

But after. Ah, then! That would be a different story.

'Here's all my love birds,' cried Lady Godolphin, waddling into the room and dispensing an aroma of bonhomie and musk. 'Oh, what a pretty necklace, Annabelle,' said her ladyship, coming closer to examine the jewels. 'Antique, I see. Is it Middle Evil?'

'No, my lady,' said the Marquess, 'I think it is a copy of a Renaissance design. It is only about a hundred years old.'

'I have some Running Essence earrings which will go very well with that,' said Lady Godolphin. 'You may have them as a wedding gift. Has Colonel Brian called?'

'Not as far as I know, my lady,' said Annabelle, flashing Minerva a mocking look.

Minerva frowned back in a warning kind of way. Lord Sylvester thought, 'Minerva has told that little minx of a sister of hers about Colonel Brian's marriage. Oh, dear vicar, where are you with that horsewhip of yours? And why do you always only *threaten* to use it? My friend's heart is shortly to be smashed and there is nothing I can do but watch.' Lord Sylvester stood lost in thought while the others chatted around him. The Reverend Charles Armitage was an amazingly perceptive man, he reflected. He was often self-centred to a fault. His religion was more fox-hunting than Church of England. But he did seem to have an uncanny knack of handling his daughters.

Annabelle chattered brightly, fighting her awakened conscience. She calmed it by vowing to try to make the Marquess a good wife.

She would steal what moments she could in Lord Sylvester's company, surely not too much to ask of the fickle gods, and that way her days to come would not be plagued by overmuch guilt.

She schooled herself to watch Lord Sylvester only when she was sure she herself was not being observed. Often his green eyes met hers with that strange unwinking catlike stare of his.

The wedding was still two whole weeks away. No need to worry about it now.

But somehow after that night the days streamed past, multi-coloured days full of pinnings and fittings and bustle. Mr and Mrs Armitage and the rest of the girls arrived, creating more turmoil. Again, Annabelle found herself always surrounded by people when she was with her fiancé, and she only caught a few rare glimpses of Lord Sylvester, but they were enough to fuel her passion, his very absences making her heart quite crazy.

She thought about him and dreamed about him constantly.

Even the wedding rehearsals in St George's, Hanover Square, had a strange dreamlike feeling.

The church is massive, square and ugly with a steeple placed above a Greek portico. But the aristocracy considered it the *only* church to be married in – that is if one insisted on being married in church. It was here in 1791 that the elderly Sir William Hamilton married the beautiful Emma Hart, the daughter of a blacksmith, entirely illiterate, who passed from one lover to another and was finally sold to Sir William by his nephew Charles Greville. But Sir William did marry her, and, to Emma at twenty-six, the marriage to her elderly diplomat must have appeared the culmination of her life. But she was to go on to scandalize the nation by her affair with Lord Nelson to whom she became 'my dearest beloved Emma and the true friend of my bosom.'

Hanover Square itself, although nearly a hundred years old – it was built in 1718 – was considered a fashionable and modern address.

Fashionable London was already beginning to move westward when George I arrived from Germany. The district west of Regent Street was still being spoken of as 'suburban territories' when the Square was built and named after the first Hanoverian monarch.

Not so far beyond the confines of the square sprawled another world of poverty and violence and disease, but the Armitage family were protected from this by virtue of their elegant place of residence.

Madame Verné's establishment was up two flights of stairs in Piccadilly, not far from Watier's, that famous Dandy club where Brummell and his cronies were to be found.

It was perhaps fitting that the well-known dressmaker should have her business in a street named after a fashion.

In the reign of Charles I, wrist bands made of pointed lace known as peccadilles were very fashionable. And Piccadilly gets its name from a shop in that famous thoroughfare where peccadilles were sold.

Unlike some other famous society dressmakers, Madame Verné did not believe in wasting money on expensive surroundings and her little showroom was stark in its simplicity.

Annabelle would have liked Madame Verné to attend her at Hanover Square, but Madame Verné, since she was to furnish the bridesmaids' dresses as well as the bride's gown at top speed, preferred the Armitage sisters to come to her. Annabelle was impressed by the various other

81

grand ladies who came to call, and would have liked to appear dignified, but it was very hard with Deirdre and Daphne romping around, giggling and sticking each other with pins, and Frederica perpetually wailing that she wanted to go home.

To Annabelle, the day of the wedding meant all the world to her. It was to be her debut, her performance of a lifetime. And although she would not be one of the unfortunates who were married off to old men for their title and wealth against their will, she was marrying for the reason that most young girls of her age married; apart from the overriding one of jealousy it was the only career open to a woman.

To marry well was to succeed in life. And like most girls of her age and upbringing, she never paused to consider what marriage really entailed.

Young ladies of the gentry and the aristocracy could be excused for not considering their future married lives to hold any fears of claustrophobic intimacy.

A gentleman's life was full of interests which did not include the society of women – cock fighting, prize fights, hunting, curricle races, clubs and coffee houses and gambling, and fashionable courtesans and politics.

One merchant, anxious to emulate the ways of society, but unwilling to keep a fashionable courtesan, went so far as to make his wife appear to be his mistress, and they spent many happily married years each playing their strange roles.

Virtue was not fashionable. To be Exclusive was all. The fear that Britain might find herself in the throes of a revolution such as had happened in France had gradually ebbed away and so the absentee landlords were back at the gambling tables, throwing away money that should have gone into their lands and property.

From time to time, both gentleman and ladies alike were reminded of the realities of the outside world. Every time there was another victory in Spain, the mob would take to the streets, discharging firearms, overturning coaches and setting them alight, and attacking any houses that did not

82

have lamps or candles shining in celebration – for there was a war party and an anti-war party in Parliament and the mob could gain easy money, hurling stones in support of the one or the other.

It was not fashionable to work, and from the floor of Almack's to the bow window of White's, one fought for a place among the ranks of the elegantly idle.

The monarchy was toadied to, but generally despised, thanks to the rise in literacy, the wide distribution of newspapers, and some of the most brilliant and cruellest caricaturists who ever lived.

The Prince Regent was Prince Florizel no more. Fat and florid, famous for his penchant for ageing mistresses and his enormous backside in skin-tight breeches, he was criticized mercilessly, perhaps because he quite obviously minded the criticism so much.

His brothers were accounted a disgrace.

The Duke of York caused a scandal when it was found out his mistress was selling commissions.

The Duke of Clarence, when a sailor, ignored his superiors' orders. In civil life, he talked like a groom, and lived with his actress friend, Mrs Jordan, who fathered him a whole brood of little Fitzclarences.

The Duke of Kent was a socialist, a radical, and intrigued against the Prince Regent. He was a military martinet who caused a mutiny in Gibraltar over the severity of his discipline.

The Duke of Sussex was foolish and extravagant; the Duke of Cambridge, eccentric, wild, and with a loud bellowing voice. The only thing to be said in his favour was that he begat only legitimate offspring.

The Duke of Cumberland was so bad that his own family spoke of him with horror. He goaded his Roman Catholic valet by sneering at his religion until the man hacked at him with a sabre, exposing the Duke's brain and making his evil face even more sinister. He survived the attack.

It was a world of double standards, of gross brutality mixed with refinement. One paid lip-service to the Ten Commandments, but the unwritten commandment, Thou

Shalt Not Be Found Out, was the one everyone bowed to. A married lady could have an affair, provided she were discreet. To be found out meant social ruin.

Minerva had been better equipped to deal with this mad world during her debut, armed as she had been with rigid Christian principles. Annabelle, with her craving for attention, her jealousy, her immaturity, and her intense calf love for Lord Sylvester, was completely bewildered.

She still wanted to put Minerva's classical nose out of joint. She dreamed feverishly of the murmur of admiration which would greet her own appearance at the church, and how Minerva would have to stand in the shadow of her, Annabelle's, radiant beauty.

Her wedding gown, emerging from under the skilled hands of Madame Verné, seemed depressingly simple, being of white satin, fastening under one arm, with a half train and a long veil of Valenciennes lace.

But Annabelle's disappointment in her gown fled before Minerva's news that her own, presented by the Duchess, was old and fussy, 'and the lace quite yellow'.

'Oh, how can you *bear* it, Merva?' asked Annabelle, round-eyed.

'I am marrying the man of my choice,' smiled Minerva, 'so I can be quite happy in whatever I have. Sylvester will not mind.'

'Aha!' thought Annabelle. 'The exquisite Lord Sylvester not mind?' It just showed how naïve Minerva was.

Minerva had thought she had discussed her honeymoon plans with her sister, but, in fact, she had neglected to do so. And so to Annabelle the Season stretched in front of her with dreams of Lord Sylvester's tall figure partnering her in the waltz.

At last the great day arrived. Annabelle was feeling all the calm of a soldier when he at last finds himself in the thick of his first battle.

Anticipation and dread had fled to be replaced by a

heady excitement. She knew she had never looked more beautiful, and that Minerva, in her fussy, yellowing lace and large feather hat, had never looked more plain.

Swelling with pride, the vicar of St Charles and St Jude led his two daughters up the aisle. Through the lace of her veil, Annabelle could see all the faces covertly turned in her direction. The whole of society was there. Familiar figures from Hopeworth seemed to spring out the crowd. There were Emily and Josephine, giggling and whispering, Squire Radford, small and frail, Lady Wentwater in a huge Bonaparte bonnet. Even the famous leader of fashion, Mr George Brummell, was there, surveying the congregation with his 'small grey scrutinizing eye'.

There was the Duchess of Allsbury, looking sour, and submitting to the fact that the marriage of her son was almost a *fait accompli*.

And being the cynosure of all this distinguished congregation intoxicated Annabelle's young senses.

After the wedding would come the London season which began in April, balls and parties with herself and Minerva and Lord Sylvester and the Marquess appearing together, always envied.

So elated was she, so determined to play her part to the hilt, that she did not even spare Lord Sylvester a glance but smiled shyly at the Marquess in a way which she was sure was exactly how a bride should smile.

But then the wedding service began.

Annabelle felt the cold chill of reality strike into her very soul.

She had heard the wedding service many times when her father married couples from the village of Hopeworth. But never had the words had such meaning, held such awful weight.

'To have and to hold from this day forwards, for better for worse, for richer for poorer, in sickness and in health, to love and to cherish, till death us do part, according to God's holy ordinance; and thereto I plight thee my troth.'

The church did not make any allowances for extramarital lusts. With every word of the service, she felt the

85

strong iron bands of matrimony fastening about her.

Then the Marquess's voice, husky with emotion, saying, '... with my body I thee worship.'

Bewildered, stricken, frightened, Annabelle trembled at her new husband's side, and for the first time thought of the night to come and the days to follow.

The bells rang out, their sound noisy and jumbled like the thoughts in Annabelle's head, when she was finally led down the aisle as the Marchioness of Brabington.

It was Minerva's moment of triumph, although she was aware of nothing else but the warm feel of her husband's hand in her own.

Her radiance and beauty transcended the fussiness of her dress. Behind her walked Annabelle, veil thrown back, eyes wide and hunted.

Her mind craved the reassurance, the justification, that she had not inflicted all this on herself. Why should *she* feel such dreadful pangs of conscience, when everyone knew that most married couples in society cordially loathed each other, and quite a number of them lived separately.

Divorce was very rare, but separation was extremely fashionable and tonnish.

But the words of the wedding service, the *commitment* to marriage, lay heavy on her soul.

The wedding breakfast was held at the Duke and Duchess of Allsbury's town house in Grosvenor Square. Annabelle listened dully to the speeches and the noise and laughter that rose and fell about her.

Snatches of conversation reached her and then her fright made her deaf to the rest. She drank a great deal of wine, until her husband gently put a hand over her glass, and she trembled before this first sign of marital authority.

The Duchess of Allsbury, who seemed determined to pretend it was a mere social gathering and no one was getting married at all, was complaining bitterly about the prison conditions in which Leigh Hunt, editor of *The Examiner*, was living. It was not that they were harsh, it was that they were ridiculously cosy, was the burden of her grace's complaint.

Leigh Hunt had been imprisoned the year before for pointing out in *The Examiner* that the Prince Regent was 'a violater of his work, a libertine over head and ears in debt and disgrace, a despiser of domestic ties, the companion of gamblers and demireps, a man who has just closed half a century without one single claim on the gratitude of his country or the respect of posterity.' It was said that Mr Hunt's cell was 'papered with trellised roses, the ceiling painted with sky and clouds, the windows furnished with Venetian blinds, and an unfailing supply of flowers.' He was also allowed his books and piano.

'Which is ridiculous,' said the Duchess, 'after what he said about our dear Prince Regent.'

'What was he charged with?' asked Lady Godolphin, who rarely read anything in the newspapers other than the war reports.

'Sedition,' said the Duchess in awful tones.

'Dear me!' said Lady Godolphin. 'Wouldn't he marry the girl?'

But Annabelle lost the thread of that conversation. She was staring down at her husband's square strong hands. Soon he would have licence to do what he wanted. 'Licence my roving hands and let them go, Before, behind between ...' Lord Sylvester was laughing at something Minerva said. He was cool and elegant as ever, long, white, almost feminine hands holding the wine glass. 'If only I could be Minerva. If only I could have married Sylvester,' thought Annabelle, and closed her eyes as a sudden wave of pain washed over her.

'Are you feeling faint?' came the Marquess's anxious voice.

'No,' whispered Annabelle. 'I-I have had too much to drink.'

To Minerva, the wedding breakfast seemed interminable; to Annabelle, it was all too short.

Minerva and Lord Sylvester were to leave first. Minerva folded her arms around Annabelle and hugged her tightly. 'I *shall* miss you, Bella,' she said, her large grey eyes swimming with tears. 'But I shall write every day.'

Annabelle gave her sister an impatient little push and stood back.

'Don't talk fustian, Merva,' she said. 'Why should you bother to write from St James's when we shall practically be living next door? You silly goose! We shall be together almost every day of the Season.'

'But I *told* you,' said Minerva desperately. 'Sylvester and I are going to Naples to start our honeymoon. We leave *now*. I ...'

A group of laughing guests broke into between them, forcing Minerva towards the door of the hall where Sylvester was waiting.

Minerva stared back at Annabelle, saw how her sister's shocked eyes flew to Lord Sylvester's, saw all the love and longing there. And then Sylvester had an arm around Minerva's waist and was leading her from the house.

'Annabelle looks as if she has seen a ghost,' said Squire Radford from his seat in the shadows of the hall. The vicar turned and looked down.

'Maybe I should have stopped it, Jimmy. Let us get away from these poxy guests and find us a decent bottle of port. I have need of your advice.'

'Do you never ask your Maker for advice?' asked Squire Radford with a flash of humour lighting up his old eyes.

'Oh, I leave my calling card quite frequently,' said the vicar. 'But you know what the Bible says, "Help yourself, and heaven will help you".'

'Jean de la Fontaine said that.'

'Who's he?'

'A French gentleman, famous for his fables.'

'Like that Greek chap Edwin's always prosing on about?'

'Aesop?'

'Him.'

'Yes.'

'Well, that's foreigners for you.' He cocked an ear. 'She's off!'

There came a terrible banshee wailing from the Square outside.

'Merciful Heavens! Who is it?'

'My wife.'

'Then don't you think we ...'

'No,' said the vicar. 'She's enjoying herself. Having the Spasm of all time with the flower o' London society to see her. Come along Jimmy.'

The two gentlemen found a quiet morning room on the ground floor with windows overlooking the gardens at the back. A gentle drizzle was beginning to fall, blurring the windows. The vicar rang the bell and ordered a bottle of port and asked for the fire to be lit for the day had become chilly.

Squire Radford settled himself in a chair on one side of the fire and the vicar sat facing him in the other. The Squire was a gnarled little old gentleman with thin stick like legs encased in clocked stockings and ending in large buckled shoes. His feet barely touched the ground. His small head was covered, or *shaded* rather, by an enormous, elaborately curled white wig. He wore sober black with a modest white cravat.

He looked more like a clergyman than did his friend the vicar who was sporting a sky-blue morning coat with silver buttons the size of soup plates.

'Now,' said the vicar, after the port had been brought and the first two glasses quickly downed, 'it's like this, Jimmy. I knew that there Annabelle o' mine did not give a fig for Brabington.'

'My dear Charles,' exclaimed the Squire, 'you are become over greedy in your social ambitions. One daughter married to a viscount is enough ...'

'No, no. I thought I was doing the right thing. Brabington is a fine young man. Any woman who hadn't got windmills in her head would fall in love with him. But Bella had this *tendre* for Lord Sylvester, see?'

'No, I am afraid ...'

'It's like this. All gels o' that age get hot for someone they can't have. And Bella's always been mortal jealous o' Minerva. So I thought that Brabington would soon bring her to heel. He's a soldier.'

'Dear me. And you expect him to regiment her

89

affections?'

'Put like that, it sounds silly. What troubles me is Annabelle always seemed to be the sort o' gel who should get married young. Too many dangerous hot passions churning around there. Now, I wonder if I'm wrong. If ever I saw a scared virgin who thought she'd made the mistake of her life, it was my Bella, leaving the church. And when Sylvester left she stared after him like Juliet seeing that there wood marching.'

The Squire twisted his glass and studied the ruby droplets creeping down the side. The fire hissed and smoked as the drizzle outside changed to a steady downpour.

'I shall tell you a story, Charles,' he said, in his high, precise voice. 'Although I am out of the world and buried, as it were, in Hopeworth, I was a wild young man in my youth. Several of my old cronies still live in town and refuse to accept their age. They paint like courtesans, smell like civet cats, and fight their increasing girth with Cumberland corsets. They call on me from time to time, bringing with them the gossip of the town. Quite a time ago, one such friend told me an *on-dit* which was circulating about the Marquess of Brabington.

'It seems he was much enamoured of Miss Cummings, a reigning belle some six or eight years ago. She and Brabington were expected to make a match of it. He had no money but her parents liked Brabington and were prepared to help the young couple out. He proposed and was cruelly rejected. A week later she became engaged to Lord Alistair Grant who was practically in his dotage. But very rich. Very rich, and with a title, you see.

'A week before the wedding, Brabington, he was plain Captain Peter Simpson then, inherited the marquessate and a considerable fortune. Round to his house comes weeping Miss Cummings, begging him to marry her, saying she loved him all along. "Then why wouldn't you marry me? Why do you wish to marry me now?" And she replies, all pretty innocence, that things are all changed now he has the title. He sent her to the rightabout and went out and got roaring drunk.'

'I'm surprised you heard all this,' said the vicar. 'Brabington didn't strike me as the type to broadcast his affairs.'

'He didn't. We all ignore servants and forget that they gossip just as we do and that they often have a nasty habit of listening at doors.'

'Gad's 'Oonds!' gasped the vicar. 'If my Bella opens up her mouth and says anything to imply she married him for *anything* other than love ... why, he'll leave her. She'll end up one o' them lost demi-widows.'

The vicar pulled a half hunter out of a capacious pocket in his waistcoat and stared at it. The wedding breakfast had begun at three. Night was pressing against the window panes. It was now ten in the evening.

'When do you think he'll try to mount her?' he said.

'Really Charles,' said the Squire with a fastidious shudder. 'For a man of the cloth, you have a vulgar tongue. I think too many hours on the hunting field have coarsened your language. To speak so, and of your own daughter!'

'Well, when?' said the vicar impatiently.

'About now.'

'And ...?'

'And unless he is a man devoid of sensitivity, he will shortly be shooting from his house like a cannon ball and hell bent on getting as drunk as possible.'

The vicar sighed and moodily poked the fire with his boot.

The Squire coughed delicately. 'We could of course take the carriage and wait outside the house ... A little advice from two older gentlemen, say?'

'He'll probably shoot me,' said the vicar gloomily.

'Perhaps. Let us go.'

CHAPTER SIX

The Marquess of Brabington had kept the town house in Conduit Street much the same as it had been in the late Marquess's day.

It was tall and thin, more spacious inside than it looked out. But the rooms were sombre and dark. There were a great deal of landscapes ornamenting the walls, their canvases so badly in need of cleaning that it was often hard to tell what part of England they were meant to portray. Annabelle felt crushed, almost extinguished by the dimness and silence of the rooms. The servants were very elderly, the Marquess not having the heart to get rid of any of them. Although Annabelle had already seen the house – in the company of her mother, Lady Godolphin and Minerva – the Marquess took her over it again, apologizing for its masculine dinginess and urging her to make any alterations she saw fit.

But although he was warm and affectionate and loving, Annabelle trailed after him from room to room, like a sulky schoolchild, and, for the first time, he found to his horror he was becoming irritated with her.

Then he chided himself, remembering that she was very young and that she had just been separated from her family.

If he had taken her in his arms or had made any reference to the pleasures of the night to come, then Annabelle might have burst into tears and confessed her fears.

But his easy manner, his atmosphere of *expecting* everything to be well with her, made her lose courage.

They shared a glass of wine and some biscuits before retiring for the night. The housemaid, Betty, had been appointed lady's maid to the new Marchioness and she was so busy putting on airs in the kitchen that she almost forgot to attend to her mistress and prepare her for bed.

Annabelle sat like a statue while Betty brushed out her hair, looking so lost and miserable that the maid was at last moved to pity and exclaimed, 'Oh, Miss Bella, if there's anything you would want to know, anything your Ma didn't tell you ...'

But Annabelle only said crossly, 'You must call me my lady, Betty, and do try not to be so familiar,' and so Betty tossed her head, and went silently off to lay out my lady's night rail.

Betty at last left and Annabelle climbed into bed and lay shivering despite the heat of the fire. She had a suite of rooms adjoining those of her husband – her husband, the stranger.

Her mind seemed to fly along on different levels of thought. At the top, she was cross because Betty was untrained and should have warmed her nightgown at the fire and passed a warming pan over the sheets. On the next, she longed for Minerva, although she knew that was mad, but she wanted the Minerva who always had rescued her from scrapes in the past. Further down lurked the handsome face and figure of Lord Sylvester, forever lost. And right at the bottom, thrumming and throbbing away, the ancient fear of the virgin, lying on the edge of the unknown.

She had extinguished all the candles so that the room was dimly lit by the rosy glow of the fire.

At last the door opened, and the Marquess strode in. A spurt of flame from a log threw his great black shadow dancing over the walls.

Annabelle lay very still, rigid. She had never felt so cold, so young, so frightened. With all her heart and soul, she longed to put the clock back and find herself alone in her narrow bed in the vicarage.

He divested himself of his dressing gown. Annabelle peeped through her fingers and saw the red light of the fire shining on the muscles of his naked legs beneath his nightshirt and screwed her eyes tight shut.

He climbed into bed and she quickly turned her back on him and scrunched up into a protective ball like a hedgehog.

'Well, my sweeting,' he said in a husky voice. 'I think you should at least kiss your husband goodnight.'

A wild hope seized her that that was all he wished – one goodnight kiss. She cautiously turned around and he gathered her into his arms and pressed her cold figure down the length of his warm, hard, muscular body.

He kissed her lightly on the tip of her nose, and she could sense, rather than see, that he was smiling.

He kissed her cheeks and her eyelids and then, very, very gently, he kissed her mouth, his hands slowly stroking the length of her body.

Annabelle began to feel warm and strangely comforted. The gentle soothing kisses and caressing stroking seemed to go on and on, until she could feel a tremor of excitement beginning to invade the pit of her stomach. His mouth pressed a little harder on hers and then began moving across her lips.

The tremors of excitement built up in Annabelle, until he put one hand on her breast and buried his mouth deeply in hers. She was swept with a feeling of wild elation and moved langourously in his arms.

The Marquess raised his mouth at last, and, cradling her in his arms, he looked down at her tenderly.

Alive now with adolescent lust, shaking and eager for more discoveries, Annabelle hardly knew where she was or what she was saying. As he drew her tightly against him again, she gasped, 'Oh, Sylvester, *love me!*'

And all at once the room seemed to go cold and black.

With one abrupt movement, the Marquess swung his long legs over the edge of the bed and strode from the room, banging the door behind him.

Outside the Marquess's house in Conduit Street a closed carriage was standing under the feeble light of one of the parish lamps. In it sat Squire Radford and the Reverend Charles Armitage. They felt they had been waiting forever. The vicar pulled a silver flask from his pocket and,

94

after offering it to the Squire, who refused, he drank a great gulp of brandy. He fidgeted for some minutes and then took out a large silver snuff box like a small coffin, flicked open the lid and took a hearty pinch. He sneezed appreciatively and wiped his nose on his sleeve, cursing as the silver buttons on his cuff got in the way.

Squire Radford shuddered fastidiously and handed the vicar a clean handkerchief.

'Just think, Jimmy,' said the vicar dreamily. '*Two* fortunes in the Armitage family. I could have the finest pack in England.'

'I have always considered it eccentric for a man of your means to have a private pack. Have you not considered a subscription hunt?' asked the Squire.

'Aye, well, there you have me. Truth to tell, I could not bear all the argyfying and organization and whatnot.'

'I hope,' said the Squire, a trifle severely, 'that your efforts to save Annabelle's marriage are prompted by concern for her welfare and not by dreams of perfecting your pack at the Marquess of Brabington's expense.'

'Brabington's as brilliant a rider over a country as ever cheered a hound,' said the vicar, ignoring the Squire's last remark. 'He'll see my way of things.'

'Furthermore,' pursued the Squire, 'money is not always the answer. Take the Reverend John Russell of North Devon. You must have heard of his celebrated breed of fox terriers. Well, *they* were all bred from a little white bitch he bought from a milkman at Oxford.'

'Never heard o' him, and I'm sure it's all a hum,' said the vicar sulkily. Then his face brightened. 'I tell ee, Jimmy, I'll be glad to get shot of the metropolis. No place for a hunting gentleman. Them newspapers, too, are always sneering at the hunting clergy. And the lot of 'em are agin blood sports. Then why don't they go for the pheasants? I *hates* pheasants. They've dispossessed the fox and demoralized the country. Foxes are crafty and that's what makes the sport the greatest. Did I ever tell you about that Green Man Inn over the far side o' Hopeminster. They kept a tame fox in the kitchen to run

95

in the wheel as a turnspit. One day, Reynard gets out and plays havoc with the geese and then disappears.

'We had hounds out next day and we picked up his scent not far from the inn. He led us a thirty-mile chase across country did that fox, and then he doubles back in a great ring, dives into the inn kitchen, leaps into the wheel, and starts turning the spit as if he had never left. The hounds would have had him, but that fat cook, Bessie, she loves that fox, so she covers him with her petticoats and starts screeching and laying into the hounds with the ladle. He died of old age, did that wretched fox. T'ain't fair.'

The Squire sighed and tucked the bearskin rug closer about his legs and felt with his feet for the hot brick.

'Do you care at all for your daughter?' he demanded.

'O' course I do,' said the vicar grumpily. 'I'm out here in this demned damp night.'

'Listen!' said the Squire, raising a finger.

There was the slamming of a street door.

The vicar thrust his head out of the carriage window.

'Gone away!' he cried, espying the tall figure of the Marquess striding off down the street. He lifted the trap with his stick and shouted. 'After him, damn you!'

The coach rumbled forwards.

For some time the Marquess of Brabington was deaf to all else but the thudding rage in his ears until he became aware that he was being hailed with loud cries and halloos.

He stopped dead and turned to face the vicar who was hanging out of Lady Godolphin's carriage window.

'*You!*' said the Marquess in accents of loathing.

'Get in,' said the vicar.

'At this moment,' grated the Marquess, 'I wish to have nothing to do with either of you or your family.'

'Which is why we are here. We knew you would be leaving in a rage.'

'You *knew* ...'

The Marquess, who had been turning away, turned back, his face white and drawn in the pale blurred light

96

of the street lamp.

The vicar's head disappeared to be replaced by that of Squire Radford. 'It must seem very odd to you, my lord,' he said in his precise voice, 'but I assure you, your feelings on the matter are not original. These things do happen on the best regulated wedding nights.'

'I think you had both better explain yourselves,' said the Marquess.

'But not here,' replied the Squire. 'A bottle of burgundy in Humbold's coffee house, I think, would ease our worry and tension. Come, my dear sir.'

He swung open the carriage door. With a shrug of his shoulders the Marquess stooped, and climbed into the carriage.

Annabelle struggled awake to the sounds of a muted altercation in the dressing room next door to her bedroom.

Suddenly the quavery voice of Jensen, the Marquess's butler, rose in exasperation. 'See here, my girl,' he said. 'If my lady chooses to hire an untrained girl from the country as her lady's maid, then it is my duty to train you. We have always kept the highest standards in the Brabington household, and we do not mean to see them lowered. Now. You do not *brush* out a silk gown. It should be rubbed gently with a piece of merino kept for the purpose. My lady's bonnets should be dusted with a light feather plume. The mud from my lady's boots should be removed with a soft sponge dipped in milk. Now, you light the fire in the dressing room and sweep the hearth, and place my lady's linen before the fire to warm. Then the hair brushes should be washed in soda. Never wash combs. It splits the tortoiseshell. We will buy you a small brush especially for this duty ...'

Annabelle pulled the pillow over her head and willed sleep to descend again. But fear kept sleep away.

She was quite sure she would be banished back to the vicarage. Would he be there when she went down to breakfast? Perhaps she could have a tray sent up. Minerva had said that very few ladies rose before noon and most had something light on a tray.

She had the sickening feeling of being in deep disgrace with no one to turn to. Mrs Armitage would simply be puzzled. She would say, 'But why did you call him Sylvester when his name is Peter?' and there was no answer to that – or certainly not one that Annabelle meant to give anybody.

Betty, with a swollen and tear-stained face, eventually came in with a cup of hot chocolate which she placed on a table beside the bed. She drew the curtains and opened the shutters. Pale sunlight flooded the room, and somewhere up by the chimneys a few birds were singing.

'My lord says he will see you ... I mean, my lady ... at breakfast in a half an hour,' muttered Betty.

'Tell him I am indisposed,' said Annabelle.

Betty returned in a short time with the message that my lord too was feeling not quite the thing and therefore he suggested that my lady should join him so that they might be ill together.

'Only,' sniffed Betty, 'it sounded more like a command to me ... my lady.'

Annabelle, could only be glad that Betty's lecture from the butler had damped her usual sly curiosity. She wearily arose and suffered herself to be dressed in a high-waisted, high-necked, ankle-length gown flared at the bottom. The sleeves were puffed at the shoulder and ended at the wrist with a lace frill. It was in a golden yellow colour of straw silk. Over her shoulders she wore a patterned silk shawl with tasselled borders.

Betty was hopeless at dressing hair. Annabelle could usually manage to achieve a semblance of a fashionable style herself, but her hair had been so frizzed and teased and pomaded for the wedding that she could hardly get the brush through it, and eventually, in exasperation, she simply wound it up in a knot on top of her head.

She dismissed Betty and opened her box of cosmetics. Perhaps if she looked ill enough, he would not shout at her. She applied a thick coating of *blanc* and then carefully painted purple shadows under her eyes.

The effect looked more hideous than sickly and she was about to wipe it off when a footman scratched at the door and called that my lord was awaiting my lady.

Annabelle gave a nervous start and hurried to the door.

She followed the liveried footman downstairs, through the silent dimness of the house. For the first time, she wondered what the servants thought of the strange wedding night.

The Marquess was seated in a small breakfast room on the first floor. It was panelled with dark wood and hung with pictures of the chase. Above the fireplace, the most savage looking stuffed fox that Annabelle had ever seen – and she had seen many – glared venomously down into the gloom.

The houses opposite were slightly smaller which allowed sunlight to penetrate the bedrooms upstairs but not any of the public rooms on the lower floors.

The Marquess was dressed to go out. He was wearing a square-cut tail coat of blue wool with long narrow sleeves, slightly gathered shoulders and small rounded cuffs with biscuit colour pantaloons and hussar boots. His black hair had been arranged *à la Brummell* in a mass of artistic curls.

His snowy cravat was tied in the Irish, and his buff waistcoat unbuttoned at the top to reveal the delicate frill of his cambric shirt.

He smiled at her in a vague kind of way and then turned his attention to his newspaper again.

Annabelle, eyeing him nervously out of one blue eye, walked over to the sideboard and lifted the cover of one dish after another. She realized she was ravenously hungry. But sick people did not have healthy appetites. She sadly settled for two pieces of toast and took her place at the table.

He seemed completely at his ease, and completely absorbed in his paper. Annabelle cleared her throat several times, but he did not look up.

At last, the Marquess put down the paper and yawned. 'Oh, my poor head,' he sighed. 'Well, I suppose I must pay for my night of roistering on the Town.'

Annabelle's blue eyes flew to his in surprise, and then a wave of humiliation engulfed her. He had not even cared.

'Are ... are we going somewhere today, Peter?' she ventured.

'No, my lady. *We* are not. I have business matters to attend to. Illness does not become you. You are looking singularly horrible this morning.'

'I-I am ill,' said Annabelle defiantly.

'Which is why I am not taking you anywhere.' The tawny eyes seemed to mock her.

'I feel a trifle better,' ventured Annabelle, 'and the sun is shining and ...'

'Then you may have the use of one of the carriages,' he said equably.

'I have no money,' said Annabelle. 'So I cannot really *do* anything.'

He pulled a heavy purse from his pocket and passed it over to her. 'Use that,' he said, 'and I will make arrangements for you to draw funds on my bank.'

'Thank you, Peter,' mumbled Annabelle.

'And since we are to go about in society, perhaps we should practise the conventions at home. I will address you as my lady and you will call me Brabington.'

'It ... it seems so *cold*.'

He made no reply to this, but put down his napkin and rose and stretched.

'Good morning, my lady,' he said. He strode to the door.

'About last night, Brabington,' cried Annabelle, 'I feel I must explain ...'

'Oh, don't please talk about last night,' he said cheerfully. 'I drank more than was good for me and I shudder to think what else I did.'

He raised his hand in a mocking little salute, and then he was gone.

Annabelle sat bewildered. He did not love her. A man in love would have fumed and raged. What if ... oh, horrible thought ... what if he had not heard her mention

Sylvester's name but had merely abruptly quitted the bedchamber because he was *bored* by her inexperience.

She raised her hands to her suddenly hot cheeks. Or was he being very clever and getting his revenge by this seeming indifference? But she should be *happy* that he did not love her. For she did not love him. She loved Sylvester. She tried to conjure up a picture of Lord Sylvester's face but found she could not.

Annabelle decided she could not think any more on the problem until she had washed her hair and face.

She rang for Jensen and told him to tell Betty to prepare a hair wash. 'I had reason to send Miss Betty out to collect some items for my lady's toilet table,' said Jensen. 'She is not trained and must learn.'

'Then she will be taught by me,' said Annabelle crossly. 'Tell the kitchens I wish a wash prepared for my hair. It must consist of one pennyworth of borax, half a pint of olive oil, and a pint of boiling water. Oh, and add a little rosemary.'

When Annabelle's hair had been washed by a housemaid and a pomatum of olive oil, spermaceti, oil of almonds and essence of lemon gently rubbed into it with a warm flannel, her spirits began to recover.

Peter was piqued, that was all. She would quietly amuse herself and show him she did not care, and soon she would win him round. It was of no use being married if one had to go everywhere oneself.

After some internal debate, she sent a note round to Lady Godolphin's asking Deirdre to be prepared to go for a drive in the Park that afternoon.

By the time Deirdre hopped into the barouche beside her, Annabelle's *amour propre* was much restored, and she forebore from sending Deirdre back indoors to take down her hair and take off the huge poke bonnet with which she had chosen to grace the outing.

Annabelle had forgotten how clear and carrying Deirdre's voice could be. No sooner had they joined the line of carriages all heading in the same direction, than Deirdre began to exclaim how *strange* it was that

101

Annabelle should be free to go on a drive on the day after her wedding.

'Why not?' asked Annabelle, trying to look poised and indulgent as an older sister should.

'I thought you would be passionately wrapped in each other's embrace,' replied Deirdre.

'*On ne dit pas ces choses devant les domestiques.*'

Deirdre wrinkled up her pert nose in concentration. 'Oh, don't speak in front of the servants!' she exclaimed. 'I thought it was fashionable to just ignore them. Everyone in London speaks bad French, Bella, so you must be all the crack. I don't know why I had to slave so many hours over my grammar. They all just translate literally. I was looking at a girl's fan at the wedding reception and she said, '*Donnez-moi ça dos,*' and I hadn't the faintest idea what she was talking about until she said she meant, give it back.

'I laughed and laughed until I *choked*, and I told Sylvester and he was *so* amused.'

'If you don't keep quiet, I shall take you straight home, miss,' said Annabelle fiercely.

'I'm sorry,' said Deirdre, immediately contrite. 'I shouldn't have mentioned *his* name, for we all know what a ...'

'*Deirdre!*'

'Very well. Is your marriage one of those arranged ones after all, Bella? I would not like one of those for myself for I am deeply romantic.'

'Now I really *am* taking you home.'

'No, don't. I will be quiet. How pretty the Park looks. See the leaves are just peeping out. I would love a dress of just that colour. I was rather disappointed in the great Mr Brummell. Not *at all* what I had been led to believe. Did you see him at the wedding? His face is rather long and his whiskers are sandy. He is neither plain nor handsome. Do you think he is famous simply becaust he introduced starch to cravats, Bella?

'You know what they say,

'All is unprofitable, flat,
And stale, without a smart *Cravat*
Muslined enough to hold its starch
That last keystone of Fashion's arch.'

'I do not know,' said Annabelle repressively. 'Now, not another word.'

They had entered Rotten Row and Deirdre fell silent as she eagerly studied all the hairstyles and bonnets and dresses.

But Deirdre could never remain very silent for long. 'I say, Bella,' she began, 'I feel dowdy and countryish, and although you are wearing one of Minerva's gowns, you do not look very *tonnish*. Why is that, do you think? Perhaps we are too young. But Minerva has acquired a great air.'

'Ooooh!' hissed Annabelle. 'I wish I had never brought you.'

For she too, had been uncomfortably aware that the other fashionable ladies had a certain something which she herself lacked. Some of them were dressed in the minimum, thin draped muslin exposing glimpses of bosom and thigh. There was also something in their carriage, the way they handled their stoles and fans, that made poor Annabelle feel like a country bumpkin by comparison.

'But do look, Bella, there is a lady who is so dashing and ... oh, dear, *don't* look! Isn't that a fascinating tree over there?'

But Annabelle did look and her face went quite cold and set.

The lady was admittedly pretty and dashing enough to turn all heads. She had a ridiculously frivolous little bonnet of feathers and coloured ribbons perched on her glossy brown curls. Her round and rosy face was all dimples and creamy skin with a huge pair of sparkling brown eyes. The thin muslin of her gown revealed a pair of generous breasts, the nipples straining against the cloth.

It was her escort who made Annabelle freeze.

Beside her in a dashing high perch phaeton, handling the ribbons to perfection, sat the Marquess of Brabington.

103

As they passed the two sisters, the Marquess turned and said something to his pretty friend and she put a possessive little gloved hand on his sleeve and dimpled up at him.

'Oh, you *saw*,' whispered Deirdre.

'Oh, 'tis nothing,' said Annabelle. 'The lady is his cousin and he was obliged to show her the Fashionables.'

'His cousin? Why wasn't she at the wedding?'

'An oversight. That is why he is trying to make it up to her.'

Deirdre looked doubtful. 'What is her name?' she asked.

'I cannot remember. But Peter will no doubt remind me when we go to the opera tonight.'

'Which opera?'

'I don't know,' said Annabelle crossly. She tried to affect a worldly-wise air. 'My dear child, one goes to the opera to be *seen*, not to listen to the music.'

'I should not like that at all. But there is only one performance and that is at the Haymarket. Catalini is singing. Lady Godolphin is taking us, so we shall see you there.'

'Of course,' said Annabelle. She would ask Peter to take her. He *could* not refuse. He surely did not mean to leave her completely alone. Who *was* that woman? And so her thoughts churned and turned.

Annabelle was glad to be rid of Deirdre when she at last dropped her at Lady Godolphin's in Hanover Square.

By the time she reached Conduit Street Annabelle had somehow persuaded herself that the Marquess *had* really been entertaining a relative.

It was inconceivable that the man who had looked at her so warmly and tenderly should feel nothing for her at all.

She hovered nervously in her room, waiting for her husband to return, so that he might tell her which social event they were to attend that evening and so that she could decide what best to wear. At last, the housekeeper entered with a menu for my lady to inspect.

'It looks very well,' said Annabelle. 'You are sure there is nothing here my lord dislikes?'

'Oh, no, my lady, but seeing as how your ladyship will be dining alone, Cook wondered if you would care for any special dish?'

'Dining *alone!*' screamed a voice in Annabelle's head. But she said aloud, 'No, this will do very well. Stay! My lord told me of his engagement for this evening but it has slipped my memory.'

'My lord is attending the Duchess of Ruthfords' ball, my lady.'

Annabelle schooled her face. 'Ah, yes, of course. I was not going because I was indisposed but since I am recovered, send Betty to me, and I will join my husband at the ball.'

'Very good, my lady,' said the housekeeper. 'My lord seemed to expect you to dine at home, my lady.'

Annabelle looked at her coldly. 'Then he was much mistaken. He will be delighted to see I have recovered.'

Of course, the Marquess's servants knew all about the incident in the Park, the ones at the back of Annabelle's carriage gleefully relating the encounter.

If Annabelle had not been so buoyed up with rage, even she would have quailed before the idea of attending her first aristocratic London ball on her own. She knew that unaccompanied ladies usually arrived with some male friend or with an elderly chaperone. But she was going to meet her husband and it was his *right* to take care of her.

Then she thought that he must return home to change for the ball. She decided to sit by the window and wait. The minutes ticked away into half hours and then hours but there was no sign of his carriage rumbling over the cobbles below.

At last she rang the bell and asked Betty to find out if my lord had come home to change. Betty returned shortly with the intelligence that the Marquess had arrived back on foot an hour and a half ago and had changed and left.

Annabelle's courage deserted her. He *knew* she was not ill. He did not want to see her. If only he would ask for an explanation. She would tell him that since Sylvester was her brother-in-law, it was natural that his name should rise to her lips.

At such a moment? jeered her uneasy conscience.

She stood by the window of her sitting room, holding back the curtain, and looked through a blur of tears at the deserted street below, hoping against hope that he would return for her.

All at once, she heard a rattle of wheels and stood very still, her heart beating hard.

An open carriage passed under the window. But it did not contain the Marquess. Instead it carried two young men and two young women. They were in full evening dress, jewels blazing. They seemed very merry and carefree and the sound of their laughter drifted up to where Annabelle stood in the silent room.

She decided then and there to go, and rang for Betty and demanded to be helped into her ballgown. Annabelle had not been much in the way of noticing the misery of others, but for the first time she became aware of the maid's distress. Betty's eyes were still swollen with crying, she had lost her springy step, and her shoulders drooped pathetically.

'What is the matter?' asked Annabelle abruptly.

'Nothing, my lady.'

The uncharacteristic meekness of Betty's reply made Annabelle look at her with sudden concern.

Betty could be sly, gossipy, irritating and impudent. But she was usually happy and good-natured and she had been with the Armitage family since she was a mere ten years old.

'Sit down,' said Annabelle quietly. 'I am late already so a few more minutes won't matter. There is something sadly wrong, Betty. Tell me, there's a dear. I do not like to see you in such distress.'

Betty's mouth fell open ludicrously at this unexpected sympathy from her mistress and then she burst into noisy tears.

Throughs gasps and chokes, Annabelle was able to make out that Betty was homesick. The upper servants treated her with contempt. She longed to go back to the vicarage. She missed John Summer. John Summer was the vicarage coachman who also acted as groom, kennel master and whipper-in.

'Are you in love with John, Betty?' asked Annabelle.

'Oh, yes, Miss Bella,' sobbed Betty, forgetting Annabelle's title. 'Ever so.'

'Then dry your eyes,' said Annabelle. 'I will tell mother in the morning that when she returns to Hopeworth, she is to take you with her. There! You can be comfortable again.'

'Miss Bella!' cried Betty, beginning to weep with happiness this time. 'I'm that grateful. But it do go hard to leave you here with all these strangers.'

'I have my husband.'

'Yes, of course, mum,' said Betty, staring at the carpet.

'Well, that's settled,' said Annabelle brightly. 'Now find me that fan with the mother-of-pearl sticks that Lady Godolphin gave me.'

Annabelle was wearing the gossamer satin robe of celestial blue with the lace vandyked hem and pearl clasped sleeves which Minerva had worn on *her* first debut. She clasped the necklace the Marquess had given her around her neck, and then pirouetted in front of Betty, laughing and saying, 'How do I look?'

'You look beautiful, my lady,' breathed Betty, and Annabelle glanced at the maid in surprise, for she had expected the usual sniff, followed by 'handsome is as handsome does.'

But Betty had not the words to explain for once Annabelle was beautiful inside as well as out.

'It don't seem right you going on your own,' added Betty. 'I'll fetch my bonnet and cloak and come with you in the carriage, my lady, as far as the door.'

'No,' said Annabelle, 'that will not be necessary.'

On impulse, she gave Betty a hug, and then left the

room and made her way downstairs.

The carriage with its two tall footmen standing by the steps was waiting outside. They assisted Annabelle into the carriage, folded up the steps, and hung on the backstrap as the coachman cracked his whip.

A great deal of Annabelle's fears fell from her shoulders. She was young and she was out in the West End of London at night where the flambeaux blazed and crackled outside the great houses and the lights of the carriage lamps bobbed like fireflies through the dark.

Since her husband had already arrived, she was not asked to produce an invitation card.

She left her cloak in a downstairs ante room, squared her shoulders, and slowly mounted the curved staircase towards the sound of music from the rooms on the first floor.

She let out a little sigh of relief. The Duke and Duchess were no longer waiting to receive the guests but had joined the party in the ballroom. She could slip in unnoticed.

But members of society had started to return to town and although there were a number of the rather effete gentlemen that Annabelle had already met, their ranks had been swelled by a good few dashing gentlemen. Mr Brummell was in Town, and where Mr Brummell went, society followed. Quizzing glasses were raised in her direction, eyes stared, heads swivelled. The much chastened Annabelle did not realize that this interest was caused by her startling beauty.

Her first thought was that everyone recognized the ballgown as being the one her sister had worn last Season and she coloured and looked right and left for her husband.

She could see no sign of him and could only be glad when a thin, tall man with cavalry whiskers and stick-like legs asked her to dance. They exchanged a few pleasantries when the figure of the dance brought them together. But when they were strolling about before the next dance as was the custom, her partner said, 'May I introduce myself. Name of Bryce. There's something about you that seems deuced familiar.'

'Perhaps you know my husband,' ventured Annabelle, 'The Marquess of Brabington. In fact I wonder if you have seen ...'

Mr Bryce stood stock still. 'I say,' he said, running a finger around the inside of his collar. 'You ain't Minerva Armitage's sister, her that's married to Comfrey?'

'Yes, as a matter of fact I ...'

'The devil!' he exclaimed. 'I don't want a cold ball of steel put in *me*.'

'I do not understand,' said Annabelle.

'Oh, *you* know, Comfrey fought a duel with Mr Dubois over your sister. I was Mr Dubois' second. I must say it was the neatest bit of shooting I ever did see. Comfrey shot the pistol right out of his hand!'

'My sister told me nothing of this!' Annabelle looked at him wide-eyed.

'May I have the honour?' A young man with a cheerful face and curly hair had stopped beside Annabelle. The next dance was just being announced. Mr Bryce surrendered her to her new partner with a patent air of relief, and Annabelle watched him as he walked off to join a group of men and began talking busily.

A duel fought over Minerva, the respectable Minerva, thought Annabelle in amazement. And she never said a word!

She felt a pang of jealousy and tried to conjure up the face and figure of beloved Sylvester in her mind.

But at that moment, she saw her husband.

He was dancing with a pretty, dark-haired girl. She was laughing and gazing up into his eyes. He looked easily the most handsome man in the room, his evening dress moulded to his tall body. The romantic image of Lord Sylvester shimmered in Annabelle's brain and was gone.

She kept looking over at her husband, willing him to notice her, and answering her partner's questions mechanically.

At that moment, Sir Guy Wayne emerged from the cardroom and leaned against a pillar and surveyed the dancers. He had a handsome dissipated face and hard mocking eyes. He wore his hair powdered, despite the fact that that fashion had largely gone out of style, thanks to the iniquitous flour tax.

He was in his thirty-eighth year and had never married. His fortune was small but his skill at cards was great, and so he was able to live comfortably on the follies of others. He had never lacked female companionship, specializing as he did in discontented young wives.

He raised his quizzing glass and studied Annabelle for several moments. At last he became aware that his friend, James Worth, was standing at his elbow.

'Who's the blonde beauty?' he drawled, waving his quizzing glass in Annabelle's direction.

James Worth gave an effeminate titter. 'That's the new Marchioness of Brabington,' he said. 'Quite pretty – if you like Dresden.'

'Oh, I do. Very much. See how her eyes keep following her husband. And see how the brave Marquess is somehow well aware that she is there and yet will not look,' mused Sir Guy. 'I think I see sport.'

'They were wed *yesterday!*' exclaimed Mr Worth.

'Definitely not a love match,' said Sir Guy, tapping the end of his quizzing glass against his teeth. 'On his side anyway. Brabington was always a cold fish.'

'I would not meddle with Brabington,' cautioned Mr Worth. 'You know what these great hairy impetuous lumps of cannon fodder are like. Always challenging one to a duel on the slightest pretext.'

'No one has ever challenged me to a duel,' said Sir Guy, his pale eyes fastened on the dancing figure of Annabelle. 'I am too discreet and I do not philander unless I am sure the husband is disaffected. In this case, I think I would try to make trouble whatever Brabington may feel for her. I wish revenge on him.'

'Faith! How Gothic you sound! I never credited you with such strong feelings. Why? What happened?'

'It was some years ago. I was playing cards at the Bell at Newmarket after the races and was just removing the last

110

of young Evanton's fortune from him when Brabington leaned forward and snatched my cards and ran his thumb over them.

'He called out that they were marked, and before I could protest my innocence, he picked me up and carried me out to the duck pond and threw me in.'

There was a silence.

'My dear friend,' said Sir Guy gently, 'I have just told you of my dire humiliation. Have you nothing to say?'

'Were they?'

'What?'

'The cards. Were they marked?'

'Such a question from such a friend,' said Sir Guy, swivelling and fixing Mr Worth with a hard stare.

'I say, I am sorry,' babbled Mr Worth. 'I don't know what came over me.'

'Don't say anything like that again,' said Sir Guy pleasantly, 'or I shall have you horsewhipped within an inch of your cringing, miserable life. Do I make myself clear?'

'Oh, yes. *Very.*'

'Now what shall I do with the fair Marchioness, I wonder? Hurt wives or bored wives like to philander or gamble. Either would do.'

'She is a vicar's daughter.'

'That does not endow her with any virtue, mark you. All our beloved clergy care about are their hounds and horses. I have yet to meet a man of the Anglican church who had a mind above the material things of life. Shall I ask her to dance? Ah, no. Her husband has deigned to notice her. Let us watch.'

The Marquess of Brabington bent over his wife's hand and deposited a kiss somewhere in the air two inches away from it.

'You must forgive me, my lady,' he said, 'I was so sure you were indisposed. And who shall blame me for thinking thus? That terrible white mask glaring at me across the breakfast table, those staring reddened eyes, those ...'

'It pleases you to jest, Brabington,' rejoined Annabelle

111

in a thin little voice. 'I am persuaded you know very well that I was not ill.'

'But you told me you were,' pointed out the Marquess. 'I trust your memory is not failing you. If you cannot remember things you say or things you do, you must write them down. Ah, we are about to begin. A Scotch reel. Splendid!'

He whirled Annabelle off into the dance at a breathless pace. There was hardly any opportunity to talk, as they were constantly being separated by the figure of the dance. The Marquess began an infuriating conversation as if there were no interruptions.

'You know, my lady ...'

Pas de bas

'... that girls of your age ...'

Figure eight

'... are subject to the strangest humours which ...'

Pass and repass

'... Lady Godolphin would no doubt describe as a load of follicles. Nonetheless ...'

Hands down the middle

'... since my time is too much taken up with affairs of ... er ... business, I would feel happier if you ...'

Grand chain

'... would consult a physician.'

And so it went on, Annabelle finding that as soon as she was about to reply, the dance separated them again.

She gritted her teeth and decided to seize her opportunity when the dance was over.

But no sooner had she risen from her curtsey than the Marquess propelled her firmly across the floor and introduced her to their hosts, the Duke and Duchess of Ruthfords. 'Your Grace, allow me to present my wife, Lady Brabington. My dear, her grace, the Duchess of Ruthfords. Ruthfords, my wife. The Duke of Ruthfords.'

'You are from Berham county, I believe,' said the Duchess, fixing Annabelle with a frosty stare. 'How is old Osbadiston?'

To Annabelle's fury, the Marquess had put an arm

around the Duke's shoulder and was strolling away.

She forced herself to reply to the Duchess's questions, and then turned in relief as a handsome and dissipated man came to claim her hand for the next dance.

'My name is Wayne,' he said. 'Your Grace will surely give me permission to dance the waltz with Lady Brabington?'

The Duchess gave a chilly nod. Annabelle had been taught the waltz by Minerva, but this was the first time she had danced it with a man. It was all very shocking having a man's hand at your waist in the middle of a room full of people. She should have been dancing this with her husband. But at least, he would not be dancing it with anyone else. And then Annabelle's blue eyes widened with shock. For the Marquess was swinging a very dashing matron into the waltz and he was holding her *much* too closely.

Anger blazed up in Annabelle and she gave her partner a radiant smile.

Sir Guy smiled back. 'You should not look at me *so*, Lady Annabelle,' he said in a mocking, caressing voice, 'or I shall be in danger of forgetting you are newly married. You are by far the most beautiful creature I have ever seen.'

'Really, sir, you exaggerate,' said Annabelle, although his compliment was balm to her wounded soul.

'No, I never exaggerate,' he said lightly. Despite her pain, Annabelle was beginning to enjoy herself a little. He was a beautiful dancer. He was older than her husband, thought Annabelle, stealing a look at him from under her eyelashes. But he was exciting with his worldly manner and his pale, almost colourless eyes which surveyed her so mockingly from under their heavy lids. His nose was straight and thin, and his mouth small enough to be fashionable with well moulded lips. His skin was very white, like coarse grained parchment, and he wore no paint. He gave her, somehow, a feeling of danger, an awareness of another world of infinite sophistication. She began to forget about her husband for quite two minutes at a time.

'I would beg you to go for a drive with me tomorrow,' said Sir Guy, 'But, alas, one so fair and so lately wed will be doing that most unfashionable of all things, going everywhere with her husband.'

At that moment, the Marquess smiled quite bewitchingly at his partner and Annabelle gritted her teeth.

'We go our own ways, sir,' she said lightly. 'If you would care to call for me on the morrow, I should be pleased to accompany you.'

'I consider myself the most fortunate of men. I will be the envy of the ton.'

'You flatter me too much, sir.'

He briefly held her a little more tightly. 'On the contrary, my lady, I tell only the truth.'

When they were walking about after the dance, Annabelle forced herself not to look around for her husband. 'I trust you have no wife, sir,' she said.

'No, I have never seen any woman who could keep my interest above a fortnight.'

'Then I shall enjoy your company while I may,' laughed Annabelle.

'We shall see,' he replied. Annabelle's hand was claimed for the next dance and she soon began to worry about something else. She was extremely hungry. Couples were drifting towards the supper room from which wafted a tantalizing smell of food. Her stomach gave a great rumble which she hoped was drowned by the sound of the music.

Her husband should have been on hand to take her to the supper room, she thought angrily. And where had he gone? For there was now no sign of the tall Marquess.

Her partner on this occasion was a Mr Bassington. He was a shy young man with a hesitant manner and rather unprepossessing features, but when he stammered out that he would deem it an honour to escort my lady to the supper room, Annabelle glowed at him as if he were an Adonis.

114

Feeling quite faint with hunger, she watched as he heaped her plate with Westphalia ham and slices of reindeer tongue, cauliflower and sausages. With a great sigh of satisfaction, she raised her fork.

'Up. Up. Up, and away!' said a voice at her ear. Her husband was smiling down at her, weaving slightly. He seemed to have become suddenly and inexplicably drunk.

'But I am about to eat, Brabington,' said Annabelle in exasperation.

'Mr Bassington – oh, *this* is Mr Bassington. Mr Bassington, my husband. Mr Bassington and I were ...'

'Were *what*?' demanded the Marquess with sudden truculence, his tawny eyes boring into Mr Bassington's quivering face.

'Nothing!' gasped Mr Bassington, looking desperately from one to the other. He rose to his feet, nearly knocking over his chair in his haste. 'I'm off!'

'Come along, my dear,' said the Marquess in a loud voice. 'You must not eat and eat and eat all day long or I shall have to put you on a strict regime of boiled potatoes and vinegar.'

He put an arm under her elbow and hoisted her to her feet.

Annabelle realized that the only way to prevent a scene was to go with him.

With one last longing look at her untouched plate of food, she allowed herself to be escorted out of the house and into the carriage.

She rounded on her husband as soon as they were seated. 'Well, sirrah,' she said, 'I trust you enjoyed your drive this afternoon?'

Snore.

She stared at the Marquess in disbelief.

His face illumined by the bobbing carriage lamps showed he had fallen neatly asleep.

Furiously, Annabelle poked him in the ribs with her fan. He went on slumbering gently.

When they arrived home she snapped at the footman, 'Rouse your master,' and holding her head high, she

115

marched into the house.

But as she ascended the stairs, a mocking voice began to sing behind her.

'Oh, Annabelle, fair Bella,
Oh, turn and let me see
Thy shining, saucy, wanton face,
Thy delicate dimpled knee
Thy ...'

'Enough,' said Annabelle, over her shoulder. 'Have consideration for the ears of the servants.'

'I do not sing loud enough?' came the Marquess's tipsy voice. 'Then that can be remedied. I will begin again.' And he began to sing at the top of his voice.

Annabelle clapped her hands over her ears and fled.

'A chase!' whooped the Marquess, pounding up the stairs after her.

He caught up with her at the door of her room and swung her round to face him. She tried to push him away but he clipped her hands behind her back.

'You are very beautiful,' he said softly, 'whoever you are.' He looked at her with a puzzled frown. 'Where did we meet?'

'Let me go! I am your wife,' said Annabelle, near to tears.

'Then I will kiss you.' He pulled her suddenly into his arms and kissed her long and langourously.

Annabelle, who had decided to submit to the kiss rather than enrage this madman, found herself caught up in a wave of hot excitement. Her lips had begun to part, to open under his, when he suddenly released her, and clapped a hand to his forehead.

'By George, I'm tired,' he said. 'Better go to bed.' And he strode off down the corridor without a backward look.

Annabelle leaned weakly against the door. How on earth had he managed to become so drunk in such a short space of time?

Betty was sitting waiting up for her. The bed and

116

Annabelle's nightdress had been thoroughly warmed, and the toilet table carefully arranged.

'I am a little shaken, Betty,' confided Annabelle, as the maid helped her out of her gown. 'My lord is in his altitudes.'

'Gentlemen are often so, my lady,' said Betty, reaching up to take the pins out of Annabelle's hair.

'Are they really? Is your John thus?'

'Only very rarely, my lady.'

Annabelle looked around the carefully arranged room.

'You have done very well, Betty,' she said. 'Are you sure you do not wish to stay?'

'Oh, I'm that torn,' sighed Betty. 'I want to go to Hopeworth, that I do, but I don't want to leave you here.'

'I shall do very well, Betty,' said Annabelle. 'I will take you round to Lady Godolphin's in the morning and tell mother to prepare to take you with her. She will be very pleased to have you back, Betty, and so will the girls.'

Betty looked curiously at her mistress, noticing the sadness in Annabelle's large eyes. It would be a terrible shame, thought Betty, if all those rumours that had been circulating at the vicarage turned out to be true, that Miss Bella was in love with Lord Sylvester and had only married the Marquess because she couldn't get him. But something *had* to change Miss Bella, something had to happen to make her grow up. The Annabelle of only a week ago would not have noticed or troubled about her, Betty's, distress.

She asked Betty to rouse her at ten so that they might proceed after breakfast to Lady Godolphin's home. Annabelle fell wearily back against the pillows and searched in her mind for one of those rosy fantasies about Lord Sylvester. But it all seemed so remote. Instead, she seemed to be back in the library at Haeter Abbey with the Marquess while the snow fell outside. His eyes were warm and golden and full of love.

She fell asleep despite her hunger pangs, with a niggling uneasy thought that she had lost something very precious but was not quite sure what it was.

117

CHAPTER SEVEN

Since she first met Lord Sylvester, Annabelle's every waking thought had been of him. But this morning, she found her one waking thought was to try to catch her husband at breakfast to see if he could explain his behavior of the night before. And did he mean to ignore her? She must explain away that dreadful use of Lord Sylvester's name on their wedding night. But how could she explain it?

Betty was all smiles, now that her London ordeal was nearly at an end. She bustled efficiently around the room and soon had Annabelle attired in a pretty sprigged muslin.

The Marquess of Brabington was just finishing his breakfast as Annabelle entered the room. He smiled at her vaguely and put down his napkin.

'Well, Brabington?' said Annabelle, in what she hoped were dowager tones. 'How are we this morning?'

'*I* am in fine fettle,' he said politely. 'As to how *you* are, my lady, I fear I do not know.'

'You were very drunk last night.'

'Indeed! I have no recollection of last night.'

'But perhaps you remember yesterday afternoon?'

He smiled a singularly sweet smile. 'Ah, yes,' he said. 'How could I forget?'

'The charms of your inamorata were perhaps more memorable than mine.'

'I think it is, perhaps, that she never forgets who I am,' he said reflectively. 'But I shall take you driving this afternoon, my lady, and perhaps we can endeavour to repair both our memories.'

Annabelle flushed guiltily. 'I fear I have made other arrangements. A certain Sir Guy Wayne was kind enough to ...'

'Then that leaves me free for other pleasures.' He rose to

118

his feet.

'Stay!' said Annabelle desperately. 'There is something I must explain ...'

His eyes mocked her and she found she could not go on. He bent over her hand and said, 'I hoped to proceed in your affections, but old and infirm as you now see me, I have no other way of avoiding the force of such beauty but by flying from it.'

And with that, he quit the room.

Annabelle had a sudden longing to burst into tears. Then anger began to mount in her. He was determined to. show the world he did not care a fig for his bride. He would find that two could play the game. She would charm Sir Guy Wayne as he had never been charmed before.

When she arrived at Lady Godolphin's home, it was to find her mother and sisters in a welter of packing. Ribbons and laces, dresses, mantles and hats lay from one bedroom to the other in mounds of disarray.

Maids were bustling about, trying to bring order out of chaos, but no sooner had they managed to get some items into the trunks than Mrs Armitage instantly demanded they must be brought out again.

The girls and Mrs Armitage were delighted when Annabelle told them that Betty was to return with them to Hopeworth. 'That's a relief,' sighed Mrs Armitage, pushing a damp wisp of hair out of her eyes. 'For I had meant to train Hannah from the village but I am inclined to think it will take *years* to teach her how to go on. Papa has advertized in the newspapers for a governess for the girls so that they need not go to school in Hopeminster any more. The boys are to commence their studies at Eton in the autumn and Dr Brown is convinced that they will manage to pass the entrance examinations. Minerva has written such a charming letter.'

Annabelle had a bitter memory of Minerva saying she would write every day. Had she, Annabelle, managed to disguise her shock and despair when she had learned Lord Sylvester was going away? Minerva had not written to *her* and Annabelle was suddenly dismally sure it was because Minerva *knew*. She felt very small and grubby.

All Minerva's many kindnesses came back to her. How she wished she had never been so silly. Then she could have written to Minerva and asked her for her advice.

'Come into my room, Bella,' called Deirdre, 'and I will show you what Lady Godolphin has given me!'

Annabelle left her mother to her disorganized packing and followed Deirdre's sprightly figure into the girl's room which she shared with Diana.

Deirdre proudly exhibited a fan with mother-of-pearl sticks and painted with a pretty pastoral scene.

'She actually *gave* it to you?' said Annabelle. 'No doubt she will send the bill to Lord Sylvester.'

'I have no doubt she will, too,' laughed Deirdre. 'She really is the most shocking old quiz, but I must confess to an affection for her. I would certainly like to be able to attract the attentions of the gentlemen in the way she does when I am her great age. Colonel Brian is quite *épris*.'

'But not enough to marry her,' said Annabelle.

'Well, you know,' said Deirdre, 'it is all very shocking. He *is* married, you see. I know, for Lady Godolphin told me.'

'He is no longer married,' said Annabelle, forgetting her promise to Minerva.

'But how ... who told you?' gasped Deirdre.

'Minerva told me. Colonel Brian's wife died last summer and he kept it a secret, did not even have a notice of her death put in the newspapers.'

'Is *Minerva* sure of this?'

'Indeed, yes. For Lord Sylvester told her. He found it out quite by chance.'

'Oooh!' said Deirdre, delighted at such a piece of gossip.

Her cry of 'Oooh!' was echoed from the doorway, and both sisters swung round.

Lady Godolphin was standing in the doorway, her hand to her heart.

Even with her layers of paint, it was possible to see she

had turned deathly white.

'It is not true,' cried Annabelle, desperate to repair the damage she had unwittingly caused.

Lady Godolphin gave a faint moaning sound and turned and fled.

'Oh, dear,' said Deirdre, beginning to cry. 'What on earth are you going to do? If Minerva told you about Lady Godolphin, I'll bet she swore you to secrecy.'

'Be quiet,' snapped Annabelle, her face flaming.

She rose and made her way slowly downstairs, wondering what on earth she could say.

Annabelle stopped short on the landing. Lady Godolphin stood in the hall, facing Colonel Brian.

'Liar!' she was saying. 'You led me to believe you were still married. *Auditor!*'

Annabelle stood frozen to the spot. She felt she should flee, that she should not be listening, but shame and worry and fear kept her where she was.

'My sweet,' began the Colonel.

'Don't use endearments to *me*. I am no longer your sweet,' retorted Lady Godolphin, putting the back of her hand to her brow in a manner strongly reminiscent of Mrs Siddons. Annabelle let out a little sigh of relief. Lady Godolphin was beginning to enjoy the drama of the situation.

'But I *love* you,' pleaded the Colonel pathetically.

'Follicles!' roared Lady Godolphin. 'You have broke my heart.'

'Then if you will not listen to me, there is nothing left!' cried the Colonel, snatching a paper knife from the hall table and holding the point against his heart.

'No! Don't!' screamed Lady Godolphin. 'I will listen. Arthur, why did you deceive me?'

The Colonel lowered the knife. 'Until I had met you, you ravishing creature,' he said intensely, 'I had led a life of dull and blameless respectability. For the first time in my life I had a real liaison. Then my wife, poor Bertha, died. I should have proposed marriage – but I could not *bear* to let go of the ecstasy of my first illicit affair.

121

'If you spurn me, then there is nothing left for me. If you marry me, there will be no happier man in London.'

'Oh, *Arthur!*' cried Lady Godolphin, throwing herself against his slight figure with such force that he nearly shot backwards through the door and out into the street. 'Arthur, of *course* I will. I have never heard anything quite so ravaged.'

Annabelle came to her senses and skipped neatly and quietly back upstairs to Deirdre's room.

'All is well,' she sighed. 'They are to be married. Lady Godolphin has forgiven her Colonel. What a scene, Deirdre! They are very well suited! Quite like the Haymarket. He even threatened to kill himself.'

'You are lucky,' said Deirdre. 'Only imagine if she had *not* forgiven him. It would be all around the town how she found out from that well known tittle-tattle, the Marchioness of Brabington. You are a *shameless* gossip, Bella.'

'I?' demanded Annabelle furiously. '*I?* When you were *dragging* every word out of me.'

'That is not true. Don't blame me because you simply don't know how to keep a secret.'

Annabelle made a dive at her sister. Deirdre jumped over the bed to the far side, Annabelle plunged after her, and both rolled over and over on the floor, clawing and punching and kicking.

'My lady?'

Both girls stopped their fighting and sat up. Annabelle's hair was tumbled about her ears and the lace fichu of her gown was torn.

The Marquess of Brabington was leaning against the door jamb watching them, his face quite expressionless.

Annabelle leapt to her feet. 'I am sorry you find me thus, my lord,' she gasped, 'but Deirdre needs schooling. She is quite unbelievably spoilt.'

'It wasn't my fault, Peter,' cried Deirdre. 'She started it.'

'Peter?' said Annabelle awfully. 'Pray address my husband by his title in future, miss!'

122

'She may call me Peter if she wishes,' said the Marquess lazily. 'It makes me feel quite one of the family. I came to tell you, my lady, that our presence is requested this evening at the Duke and Duchess of Allsbury's.'

'What do *they* want?' demanded Annabelle rudely.

'This gets more like a nursery scene every minute,' said the Marquess coldly. 'They wish the pleasure of our company.'

Deirdre was staring, wide-eyed, from one to the other.

Annabelle flushed and bit her lip. 'Very well,' she said.

'Good, I shall expect you at eight o'clock.'

'Where?'

'At home, of course. Now I must leave. You may carry on.'

'I am not in the habit of brawling,' said Annabelle stiffly. 'The provocation was great.'

But the infuriating Marquess had left.

'You really don't like each other much, do you?' said Deirdre, round-eyed.

'That's quite enough from you, miss,' said Annabelle crossy. 'Marriage is something *you* will never understand.'

'I am sure I shall be married myself quite soon,' said Deirdre airily.

'*You!*' said the Marchioness of Brabington gathering up the rags of her dignity. 'Who on earth would want to marry *you*.'

Deirdre's mocking shout of 'Someone who *loves* me,' followed her down the stairs.

Annabelle fumed silently on the road back to Conduit Street. How could she have been so silly as to tell Deirdre the gossip about Lady Godolphin? Thank goodness, everthing seemed well in that direction. She shuddered to think what the Marquess would say if he found out.

She sent Betty away so that the maid could begin her preparations for the journey to Hopeworth, and sent for the butler, Jensen, and asked him to employ a lady's maid as soon as possible.

The butler said that a certain Lady Habbard's maid was looking for new employ and had a good reputation, and that he would try to engage her services. Then he handed Annabelle a note, said it was from the Marquess, and withdrew.

Annabelle opened it, wondering what he had to say to her that he had not seen fit to say in front of Deirdre. The note was short and curt. 'My lady,' she read. 'It is my wish that you forego your drive with Sir Guy Wayne. He is not a suitable escort. I trust you will oblige me in this matter. B.'

Annabelle crumpled up the note in a fury, and then slowly smoothed it out and read it again.

A little smile curved her lips. Peter was jealous! There could be no other explanation.

If Sir Guy Wayne were not respectable, he most certainly would not have been invited to the ball last night, thought Annabelle naïvely, unaware that the ballrooms and drawing rooms of London held a great many villains who were invited for their bloodline and not their character. She turned her attention to the little pile of cards and bouquets which had arrived from her partners of the night before. Nearly all had called in person as was shown by the neatly turned-down corner of each card.

She decided to dress with especial care for the outing.

But while she was waiting for Sir Guy to arrive, she began to experience some qualms of doubt. Just suppose the Marquess was right? Just suppose Sir Guy *had* an unsavoury reputation?

But the sight of him driving up in a swan-necked phaeton, very much a man of the world, looking beautifully tailored and urbane, put her fears to rest.

When she was seated beside him he complimented her gracefully on her gown of jonquil muslin and said she outshone the sun. Annabelle glowed at the compliment and hoped her errant husband would be in the Park to see how admired she was, and how she had ignored his letter.

It was a beautiful spring day, warm enough to feel like summer. A brisk little breeze sent the new green leaves turning and glittering in the lazy afternoon light. Annabelle felt very much on display, perched as she was on the high seat of the phaeton. She saw the Misses Abernethy and gave them a stately bow.

They had made the round and were coming back along Rotten Row at a smart pace and Sir Guy Wayne was wondering if he should squeeze Annabelle's hand, or if that move would be too bold, too soon. He had chatted to her easily and paid her many light compliments, all of which, he noticed with gratified surprise, were gratefully welcomed. He would have thought a girl of Annabelle's beauty to be quite in the way of receiving fulsome praise from a host of admirers.

They were bowling along, well pleased with each other, when Sir Guy said, 'Here come two of the most formidable patronesses of Almack's, Lady Castlereigh and Mrs Drummond Burrell.'

Annabelle sat up very straight. Vouchers to Almack's Assembly Rooms were a *must* during the Season. Any female who was refused vouchers could consider herself a pariah.

At that moment, one great yellow wheel detached itself from Sir Guy's phaeton, and, the next instant, the carriage keeled over. Sir Guy landed face down in the mud of the still spongy ground. Annabelle, who found herself shooting through the air, seized hold of a projecting branch of a lime tree with the agility of a monkey and hung there, waving her legs around looking for a foothold. Her dress had ridden up around her knees, exposing to the common gaze a very saucy pair of lace pantalettes.

Mrs Drummond Burrell and Lady Castlereigh came abreast. 'Dear me,' said Lady Castlereigh. 'Who is that gel swinging around the trees?'

'That, I believe, is the new Marchioness of Brabington,' replied Mrs Burrell with a shudder.

Both ladies turned their heads away from the offending sight, and therefore failed to notice the broken carriage which had caused the mishap.

Throwing all dignity to the winds, Annabelle wrapped her legs around the trunk of the tree and slid to the ground.

Sir Guy had scrambled to his feet and was trying to make light of things. A crowd had gathered around the broken phaeton. Someone was holding the horses' heads. The traces had been cut, and the frightened horses were still rearing and plunging. Soon the air was loud with descriptions of what had happened, what could have happened, and what might have happened.

Annabelle was jostled and pushed by the crowd. She looked hopefully in Sir Guy's direction for assistance, but he was engaged in arguing with the fellow who had caught the horses and quieted them, and who obviously expected to be paid for his trouble.

Remembering that Conduit Street was not very far from the Park, Annabelle turned on her heel and walked away.

To her relief, her husband was not at home when she arrived, looking hot and dishevelled.

The clock in the hall told her that it was six-thirty and that she had only an hour and a half to get ready to go out with her husband.

Betty and two of the housemaids worked like troopers, carrying up a bath and cans of water, washing Annabelle's hair, and running hither and thither to assemble all the things she needed for the evening.

Annabelle wondered what type of evening it was to be.

Would it be a rout, or a *musicale*? At last she decided to wear a white lingerie gown under a straw coloured tunic with a pale blue spotted scarf over her shoulders. Once again, she wore the necklace the Marquess had given her, reflecting, as she felt its weight, that there were other jewels belonging to the Brabington family, but so far he had shown no sign of giving her any more.

With Betty's help, she managed to achieve a Grecian effect by piling up her hair and threading it with thin silk ribbons.

Her eyes in the looking glass looked very dark. She painted her face delicately, no longer caring whether Betty knew she used cosmetics or not. Betty stood in open-mouthed fascination, watching Annabelle's clever hands.

At last it was time to join her husband. Annabelle found

herself feeling breathless and uneasy and wished with all her heart she had not gone driving with Sir Guy. Now she would have to face up to the prospect of a row.

Her husband was standing by the fireplace, one arm along the mantel, his eyes gazing into the flames.

He was not aware she had entered the room, and she hesitated in the doorway, watching him. He looked very handsome. His thick black hair was fashionably dressed *à la Titus*. He was wearing a blue silk frock coat with a stand-fall collar and straw coloured knee breeches, very tight and very fitting.

His white silk stockings moulded his calves without a wrinkle and his flat-pumps had small diamond buckles. Diamonds winked among the snowy folds of his cravat and sparkled on his fingers, the massive, heavy design of his rings suiting his strong, square hands.

The firelight flickered in his strange eyes, making them look topaz, somehow predatory, like the eyes of a hawk.

As he looked up and saw her he surveyed her in silence, his face quite set and grim.

And then he smiled at her. A blinding, bewitching smile, so unexpected, so devastating in its effect, that Annabelle found she was babbling out excuses. 'I-I'm so sorry, Brabington. I forgot to tell Sir Guy *not* to call, but he *did*, and y-you s-see ...'

He came forwards and took her hands. 'You look divinely,' he said. 'And I am relieved to hear that you did not really mean to go driving with Sir Guy. I had thought that you might go just to spite me.'

His voice held a faint question and Annabelle dropped her eyes quickly. 'Furthermore,' he went on when she did not reply. 'Sir Guy does not often look after his carriage or his cattle very well.'

'No,' said Annabelle. 'There was an accident. And ... and the wheel fell off. And ... and I just walked away. I was so embarrassed. Everyone was shouting and staring, and two of the patronesses of Almack's chose that very moment to drive past, and it *would* be when I was hanging from that tree ...'

127

'Let me see, I *did* hear you aright? You were *hanging* from a tree?'

'Yes, it was quite terrible. You see, I was catapulted over Sir Guy's head. He fell in the mud and I found myself flying through the air and caught a branch of a tree, and I was hanging there and Mrs Burrell and Lady Castlereigh – they did not seem to notice the accident. They looked at me in disgust, you know, and then they just turned their heads away.'

'I doubt very much whether you will be receiving vouchers for Almack's this Season, my love,' said the Marquess, trying not to laugh.

'Oh, but I *must!*' wailed Annabelle, involuntarily clutching his hands. 'I would *die* if I did not go.'

He dropped her hands, a shade of disappointment crossing his face. 'These things are very important to you, my lady,' he said flatly. 'I will see what I can do.'

'Thank you,' said Annabelle, peeping up at him from under her lashes. She wished he did not look so stern.

He seemed to recover his spirits on the road to the Duke of Allsbury's. 'What kind of entertainment is it to be?' asked Annabelle.

'We are invited for dinner. Then there will be some cards and dancing.'

'I wish, somehow, we did not have to go.'

'You forget,' he said quietly. 'They are now your sister's relatives by marriage.'

'Yes, I do forget,' said Annabelle candidly. 'They are not at all like Lord Sylvester.'

'Ah, Sylvester,' he said.

There was a little silence.

'Peter,' said Annabelle desperately. 'I should explain ...'

'Yes, I meant to ask you,' he replied. 'The day I gave you that necklace, before we were married, you suddenly said you wanted to tell me something, and then we were interrupted by the arrival of Sylvester and your sister. What was it?'

Annabelle remembered vividly that that was the very

moment she had been planning to cancel the wedding. 'I forget,' she said in a small voice.

'Then what were you about to tell me now?'

'I wanted to tell you,' said Annabelle, clasping her hands tightly in her lap, 'that ...'

At that moment the carriage door was opened and the steps let down.

'You may tell me later,' he said. 'We are here.'

The Duchess of Allsbury gave the Marquess a very warm welcome and all but ignored Annabelle. She did, however, fix her with one brief, chilly glance and asked her if she had heard news from Minerva.

'No,' said Annabelle, miserably aware that the Marquess was watching her intently. 'She has not written to me yet. I believe my mother has heard from her.'

Annabelle was then further mortified to find that Sir Guy was not only numbered among the guests but that he had been placed next to her at dinner, the Duchess firmly believing that all married couples should be immediately separated.

To her relief, he seemed in good spirits and made such a joke of the whole thing that she found herself laughing gratefully.

'But the strangest thing happened,' he went on, 'when a man came to repair the damage.

'You see, someone had *sawed* nearly through the axle. Is it not strange? Now who would wish me ill? I am such an inoffensive fellow.'

'I do not know,' replied Annabelle, casting an involuntary look in her husband's direction.

'Where was Brabington this afternoon?' asked her companion.

'I do not know that either.'

'What an odd pair of newly-weds you are,' he laughed. 'Or are you merely being terribly fashionable?'

'I do not discuss my husband,' said Annabelle, looking at her plate and therefore failing to notice the rather reptilian look which had just flicked across Sir Guy's pale eyes.

'Then we shall talk of other things,' he said lightly. He proceeded to tell Annabelle all the latest gossip. It was slightly malicious, but always amusing, and she found herself beginning to relax, to enjoy the fact that such a sophisticated man was paying her so much attention.

Nonetheless she was resolved to be an attentive and loving wife. But this transpired to be a very hard thing to do. When they retired to the drawing room and were joined by the gentlemen, the Marquess promptly attached himself to Lady Godolphin who was also one of the guests. Annabelle found herself surrounded by a small court of admirers, and, although she laughed and flirted, her eyes kept straying to where the Marquess sat in the corner. She prayed that Lady Godolphin would not tell him how she came to find out that Colonel Brian wasn't married, but, at one point, Lady Godolphin's turbaned head bent very close to the Marquess's black one and she began to whisper intensely. For a brief moment when she had finished, the Marquess looked straight across the room and his eyes locked with those of his wife, his gaze cold and assessing.

Then he turned back to Lady Godolphin and made some light rejoinder as he rose to his feet. The guests were beginning to drift through to the music room where dancing was to be held.

Annabelle became aware several gentlemen were asking her to dance. 'I don't know,' she said, still watching her husband. 'Perhaps my husband ...' And then she broke off. The Marquess was bowing in front of Lady Coombes. She smiled at him, her rather hard face softening, and she looked almost coquettish as she took his arm and allowed him to lead her through into the music room.

Rebellion surged up in Annabelle again. *Why* would he not be open with her? If he had heard aught from Lady Godolphin to make him take her in dislike, then he should *tell* her, instead of pointedly abandoning her in this public way.

The Duchess had noticed this piece of by-play and her mouth was curled in a little satisfied smile.

130

Annabelle accepted the first of her courtiers and then proceeded to flirt for the rest of the evening with all the men in general and Sir Guy in particular. The reason she singled out Sir Guy was because she already knew him. She felt *safe* with him: in her eyes he was a middle-aged bachelor.

When Annabelle was led off into a lively country dance by Mr Charles Comfrey, Sir Guy found his friend, James Worth, at his elbow.

'Well, what do you think, James?' he asked, watching Annabelle's pretty figure moving across the polished floor. 'Does the disappointed wife take the bait?'

'Oh, yes, definitely. Absolutely,' said Mr Worth.

'And yet, I am not sure,' mused Sir Guy. 'There is a certain tension between them. They are not indifferent to each other, no matter how hard they try. I took her driving this afternoon, dear James.'

'And how did that go?'

'Not at all. For the simple reason that someone had sawed a neat line in my axle so that the wheel would fall off in the most public way possible – which it did. If Brabington was behind it – and I'm sure he was – then I have one more reason to thirst for revenge. War has been declared in earnest.'

'Talking about war,' giggled Mr Worth, 'why isn't our fire-eating hero back to the wars?'

'Just married. He will return soon.'

'Then that will leave the field clear.'

'You do not understand me. I do not want an easy field. I want the so-dear Marquess right here in London so that all may witness his humiliation.'

'I' faith, you are a hard man, Guy!'

Sir Guy turned quickly away from him to bow before Annabelle, who looked as glittering as the jewels about her neck. Her large eyes sparkled like sapphires and were every bit as hard.

'Do you wish to dance?' asked Sir Guy. 'It is the waltz.'

Annabelle looked across the room. The Marquess was asking Lady Coombes to dance – again.

'No,' she said brightly. 'I think I would like some refreshment.'

'Very well.' He tucked her hand in his and led her into an adjoining room where refreshments were being served.

'Goodness, it is hot,' said Annabelle restlessly.

He handed her a glass of iced champagne which she drank thirstily.

'There is quite a pretty garden outside,' he said, leading her to one of the long windows at the end of the refreshment room which overlooked a terrace with steps leading down into the night blackness of the garden. 'Would you care to step outside with me for a little fresh air?'

'I do not know if I should. We have no chaperone.'

'You forget. You are a married lady now and may dispense with such conventions.'

He opened one of the long windows as he spoke. A damp, warm breeze blew in on Annabelle's face. She turned and looked back to the ballroom, but there was no longer any sign of her husband among the shifting throng of dancers.

She felt a dull ache in the pit of her stomach. 'Very well,' she said, 'but only for a moment.'

They walked together along the terrace and down a shallow flight of mossy steps. A faint mist lay over everything, pearling the grass and condensing in heavy drops like tears to plop from the bushes.

There was a small round pond in the centre.

'I believe it is stocked with goldfish,' said Annabelle.

'Very romantic.'

'No, I do not like goldfish. These ones are fat and vacant-eyed.'

'We should have brought some bread and fed them.'

'Stoopid!' laughed Annabelle, momentarily forgetting her woes. 'To feed fish on a damp night! We are quite mad to be promenading thus. I am sure the hem of my dress will be quite ruined. Let us return.'

'Alas, I would rather stay here. The moonlight is enchanting.'

'There is no moonlight.'

He came very close to her. 'There is moonlight in the twin pools of your eyes. Deep in the mysterious blue depths. I gaze into your eyes, Annabelle, and I feel myself drown.'

'Sir! You forget yourself. We must return.'

She was suddenly nervous. He was so close to her, she could feel the heat from his body, see the strange glitter of his eyes.

She took a half step back and he caught her hand in his.

Then Annabelle looked a little to the side of him, her fears all at once forgotten as a small movement caught her eye.

It seemed as if a long, black, thin shadow was slowly stretching out of the bush. It was like a strange branch growing towards Sir Guy.

She opened her mouth to exclaim something when the branch or pole made a sudden thrusting jab.

It caught Sir Guy full in the middle of his waistcoat, and, with a startled exclamation, he lost his footing on the wet ground and toppled backwards in the pool.

Annabelle ran up and down the edge of the pool, making little helpless cries of distress.

To her relief, Sir Guy's head appeared and he sat up, reminding her that the pool was only three feet deep.

'What the ******?' shouted Sir Guy.

'A branch pushed you,' babbled Annabelle, 'and I must go. I really *must* go. It will look very odd if we are found here like this. Do, pray, let me go into the house and send the servants.'

And paying no heed to Sir Guy's strangled shout she ran quickly up the steps, along the terrace, and, taking a deep breath, slid quietly into the refreshment room.

The sounds of voices and laughter and music poured in from the ballroom. The refreshment room was empty save for the presence of the Duke of Allsbury who was pouring himself a glass of wine.

'Your grace,' said Annabelle, 'Please send a servant into the garden. I – I was standing by the window and heard a

133

terrible splash and a cry for help. I fear someone has fallen into the pool.'

'What!' barked the Duke. 'Some fellow has become bosky again and has decided to swim with my goldfish?' I'm really tired of this. In my day, men knew how to hold their wine. Here, you!' to a footman. 'There's someone in the pool. Go and get him out.'

Annabelle waited in a fever of apprehension. It had seemed so innocent to stroll with Sir Guy in the garden. But now she could imagine the startled questions and explanations. And Sir Guy had proved to be overwarm in his attentions.

But the servant returned and said that the garden was deserted and there was no sign of anyone in the pool.

Annabelle heaved a little sigh of relief. What had happened? Had her eyes been playing her tricks? Perhaps there had been no mysterious branch at all and Sir Guy had merely lost his footing.

She glanced down at the hem of her dress and saw that it was a little damp. She slipped quietly around the edge of the music room and out and down the stairs to the ante-chamber which had been set up as a special room for the ladies to repair their faces and hair and to leave their cloaks.

An elderly maid was in attendance. Annabelle sat down in front of a looking glass and opened her reticule. If she fiddled with her hair and pretended to rearrange it for a few minutes, it would give the hem of her gown a chance to dry.

The room was divided by several screens. Behind each screen stood a toilet table and looking glass, the idea being that the ladies could paint or powder in privacy.

Annabelle took some pins and a brush from her reticule, and began to twist a few stray curls back into place.

'Well, what do you think of the Brabingtons?' came a female voice from behind another screen. Annabelle froze with the brush half way to her hair.

'Very odd,' laughed another female voice. 'Only just married and never together.'

'Well,' said the first, 'one love match for that vicarage family is surely enough. We never thought to see dear Sylvester quite so taken. Ah, but Brabington. What a man! What shoulders! And he has the best legs of any man in London!'

'Legs!' giggled the second. 'Priscilla, you are too bold. If Lord Brabington could only hear you!'

'Mayhap I shall tell him myself, and quite soon,' rejoined the one called Priscilla with a little laugh.

Annabelle sat very still. Lady Priscilla Coombes. She had recognized her voice.

All at once, the first pangs of possessiveness began to assail Annabelle. He was *her* husband, her *property*. How *dare* he rouse such ambitions in other women?

'How dare you rouse such ambitions in Sir Guy Wayne?' sneered the voice of her conscience.

'Oh, be quiet!' Annabelle said to her conscience, and a young lady who had come round the screen quickly backed away in fright.

'That's that,' Annabelle told her reflection with a sort of gloomy satisfaction, 'I hang from trees, I gossip, I fall in love with my brother-in-law, and now I talk to myself. What else?'

But the words 'fall in love with my brother-in-law' rang strangely in her ears. 'Sylvester,' she whispered. But there was no answering warmth or longing. In her mind he was a charming cardboard figure, a toy of her schoolgirl days, something once cried over with childish fervour, something now barely understood. Annabelle began to wonder if she had loved and lost – or if she had ever loved at all.

She went slowly back to the ballroom, plucking at the blue scarf around her shoulders in a nervous, unsure way, looking out at the world as if she were seeing for the first time.

There was no sign of Sir Guy Wayne. There was no sign of her husband either. An anxious Lady Godolphin came bustling up. The Marquess had searched everywhere for her, she said, and having failed to find her, had gone home.

'He said he would walk,' said Lady Godolphin, 'so you may take the carriage.'

Annabelle looked at Lady Godolphin fully for the first time, seeing the anxious worry and concern under the layers of paint.

'Thank you,' she said gently. 'Lady Godolphin. I owe you a most humble apology. I was told about Colonel Brian and sworn to secrecy. I had no right to break such a confidence. I would not cause you pain for anything in the world.'

'Well, now,' said Lady Godolphin, crushing Annabelle to a chest full of jewels. 'If you ain't the sweetest thing that ever was.

'Now if you hadn't of said all that, I wouldn't be getting married. So it all worked out for the best. God moves in mischievous ways, as your dear father would say.'

'He does indeed,' said the Marchioness of Brabington.

CHAPTER EIGHT

Somehow Annabelle was not surprised to learn that her husband had arrived home and promptly gone out again. She felt very odd, thinner, older, as if the other Annabelle, the careless, thoughtless one had left, leaving behind a pale, formless person.

She was very quiet as Betty undressed her, until she seemed to rouse herself, and said, 'You may have my pink muslin gown to take back to Hopeworth with you. You've always liked it.'

'You mean take it back for Miss Deirdre,' exclaimed Betty.

'No, I mean for you to wear,' said Annabelle. 'It would not look well with Deirdre's red hair.'

That set Betty crying. She couldn't bear to go away and leave Miss Bella alone in London. It didn't seem right. Annabelle forced herself, despite her fatigue, to soothe the maid, and eventually sent Betty away reassured.

She climbed into bed and thought about her husband. She wondered why he had married her and then she realized that he had married her for love – a love which seemed to have disappeared. She remembered the warmth of his gaze, the feel of his lips against hers, his long, hard body pressed against her own. A large tear rolled down her cheek and sparkled in the lace at the throat of her nightgown.

Perhaps tomorrow would bring some changes. Perhaps there was something she could do or say that would bring the warmth back to his eyes.

In a coffee house, not very far away, the Marquess sat entertaining the vicar, the Reverend Charles Armitage, and his friend Squire Radford.

They had talked of the war, they had talked of the economy and they had talked of the political situation until at last a silence fell on the group.

'Well,' demanded the vicar at last. 'How goes Bella?'

'Better, I hope,' said the Marquess, turning his glass in his fingers so that the diamonds on his rings winked and sparkled.

The Squire gave a delicate cough. 'And did you follow our advice and behave badly?'

'I have behaved very badly,' said the Marquess ruefully.

'And is it working?'

The Marquess looked thoughtfully at his wine. 'Annabelle is very angry, very upset, but at least I do not think I have allowed her much peace to think of anyone else.'

'That Guy Wayne is a bad 'un,' said the vicar.

'He has his uses,' said the Marquess. 'And I have made sure that he appears only ridiculous.'

'Better be careful,' growled the vicar. 'These snake-like men can strike hard and fast when you least expect it.'

'I am not afraid of him,' said the Marquess calmly. He refilled his glasses. 'What a pair of reprehensible old sinners you are,' he grinned. 'Now what gave you the idea that the ladies like villains?'

'Oh, mere observation,' said the vicar hurriedly. 'Don't play the game too long. Are you going back to the wars?'

'Not yet,' said the Marquess. 'They have given me certain duties in town. They expect me to sell out, you know.'

'And will you?'

'I don't know. When the Season is ended, I shall see. 'But,' the Marquess roused himself, 'it is time I went. Do not worry about Sir Guy Wayne. There is nothing he can do.'

The following morning brought Annabelle a letter from Minerva. She turned it over and over in her fingers, and then with an exclamation of impatience broke open the seal and read the contents, holding the letter far away from her so that any recriminations on Minerva's part might not leap off the page and stab her as painfully as they might do if she held the paper closer.

But the letter was simple and direct. Minerva apologized for not having written before. They were held at Dover since there was something about their ship which needed to be repaired and involved a great deal of nautical terms which she did not understand.

Minerva went on to talk about the happiness of marriage and the beauties of Dover. Then followed a long historical and geographical description of the town. Annabelle's eyes flew across the lines. She turned the page. 'And so, dear sister,' Minerva ended, 'you have been much in my Thoughts. Sylvester has just come to tell me we are to sail in the morning and since we shall be at sea for some long time, it will be quite a while before I can write to you again. Be happy in your Marriage, Annabelle, and cherish your husband who is a fine man and most Worthy of you. Remember, that although I do not write, you are never absent from my Thoughts. It is always best to remember that the Good Lord expects us to *cherish* that which we *have*. For if we do not, they will be Taken from us. Yr. Loving Sister.'

Annabelle let the letter drop in her lap and stared across the room with unseeing eyes.

Minerva knew. It was in that last paragraph. Minerva knew of her younger sister's infatuation for Lord Sylvester. Annabelle knew her sister too well. That which she had was clearly Lord Brabington. Except, it seemed as if she had no hold on him at all!

Sir Guy Wayne had spent a restless night after his ducking in the goldfish pool.

He wondered whether Annabelle had pushed him, or if someone or something else had thrust him backwards. He had left by the garden gate and had had to walk home in his wet clothes because he could not bear to make a fool of

139

himself in front of his own servants by waiting outside for his carriage, dripping wet, and with bits of weed hanging from his clothes.

He realized his thirst for revenge was so fierce that it was stopping him from all logical thought. Around eight in the morning he at last fell into a heavy sleep for one hour, and awoke feeling clear and confident.

He ate a hearty breakfast and carefully turned over in his mind all he knew of the Marquess of Brabington. And then he recalled a recent and fascinating bit of scandal. The Marquess was rumoured to have had a liaison with a certain high-flyer, Harriet Evans. The scandalmongers had whispered that the Marquess had been seen driving Harriet in the Park the very day after his wedding and that Annabelle had been present in another carriage with her little sister.

His pale eyes took on a shine of triumph. He would not rush into any plot, but would think of how to use this new weapon very carefully.

Harriet Evans had made the mistake of falling in love with her latest lover, a younger son with too many gambling debts and not much in funds to pay them with. Harriet was extravagant. And yet Harriet had remained peculiarly faithful to this young spendthrift. It followed that Harriet would be in sore need of money.

It was a damp, grey morning when he finally left his lodgings in St James's Street, but he felt the sun was shining on him as he cheerfully tooled his repaired phaeton in the direction of the village of Islington.

Harriet Evans lived in a pretty little villa which had the appearance of having woken up one morning to find itself surrounded with other buildings. It looked as if it ought to be standing alone in a pleasant bit of park instead of sandwiched between two tall houses in Frog Lane.

Sir Guy rang the bell and waited. The house seemed silent, although a wisp of smoke rose from one of the chimneys.

He tried the bell again but it was of one of the organ stop variety where you are never sure whether the wire you are tugging is still connected to a bell.

After some deliberation he rapped on the door with his cane, and called out, 'Halloa there?'

At last, a casement window was pushed open upstairs and a dusty-looking housemaid in a huge print mob cap asked him what he wanted.

'Sir Guy Wayne,' he replied impatiently, 'come to see your mistress.'

She looked at him doubtfully and then drew her head back in again and slammed the window.

Sir Guy forced himself to be patient. These whores kept late nights or worked all night so they were more likely to be abed at this hour than the more respectable female.

At last there came the sound of bolts being drawn back and the same housemaid appeared at the door and bobbed a curtsey. 'The mistress will see you now,' she said.

She led him into a small, overcrowded parlour and left him. He looked about curiously. Everything was very neat and clean. The little occasional tables were crammed with snuff boxes and ornaments and miniatures on stands. The walls were covered from top to bottom with oil paintings, depicting various rural scenes. One large looking glass was suspended over the crowded mantel.

He heard a light step behind him.

Harriet Evans was in her undress. A lacy nightcap balanced on her glossy, pomaded curls, and her bodice and petticoats were imperfectly concealed by a frivolous peignoir.

'Sir Guy,' she smiled, extending a dimpled little hand. 'This is an unexpected pleasure.'

'You look enchanting this morning,' he said, bending over her hand.

'And what brings you here? Pray take a seat and I will ring for refreshments. Madeira? Port?'

'Madeira will do splendidly,' he said, sitting down on a small plush chair. She arranged herself on a diminutive sofa opposite and looked at him with the open and innocent friendliness which constituted the major part of her charm.

'Are you still with young Persalt?'

'Mr Harry Persalt,' she murmured. 'Yes.'

'Good. I have a business matter I wish to discuss with you.'

A shadow crossed her face and she opened her mouth to reply, but at that moment the housemaid slouched in with wine and cakes, so Harriet contented herself by twisting the lace edges of her peignoir between her fingers until the girl had left.

As the door closed, she raised her eyes to his. 'I am no longer in the way of ... er ... business,' she said.

'The world well lost for love,' sneered Sir Guy, and then, noticing the lift of her chin and the hardening of her face, he amended quickly, 'You deserve a good and regular life, Harriet. You were made for naught else.'

'Then what is the nature of your business?' said Harriet sharply.

'I assume you have need of money.'

'Not in the least,' said Harriet with a careless laugh.

'Then there is nothing more to be said.' He sipped his madeira, watching her over the rim of his glass, like a cat watching a mouse.

An Irish drunk outside the Barley Mow public house hard by began to sing in a lilting tenor,

'Of all the girls that are so smart
There's none like pretty Sally,
She is the darling of my heart,
And she lives in our alley.'

'Pretty,' said Harriet, swinging a pink stockinged foot from which dangled a frivolous feathered slipper. 'I wonder who wrote that.'

'Harry Carey wrote it,' said Sir Guy, still watching her. 'That precious alley was in Clerkenwell. He lived in Warner Street. He was a bastard of the Marquis of Halifax.'

'It's still pretty,' said Harriet with a toss of her curls.

'So I gather you have no need to hear my business

142

proposition?' he pursued.

'Well, it depends what it is.'

'Would five hundred guineas interest you?' he asked.

She gave a scornful laugh. 'I shudder to think what I would have to do for that.'

'Simply play a trick on a friend ... an old friend of both of us.'

'There must be more to it than that. Who is this old friend?'

'Brabington.'

'Ah, there's a man,' sighed Harriet.

'You have been seen driving with him recently.'

'That's all it was ... driving. He arrived a few days ago by chance and offered to take me to the Park at the fashionable hour.'

'Did it not strike you as strange, and he so lately wed?'

She laughed deep in her throat. 'Why should it seem strange to *me* of all people? When did society ever marry for love?'

'Perhaps,' he said with a thin smile.

Harriet looked at him curiously. 'What is it you would have me do?'

'I wish you to gain an audience with his wife and tell her you are with child by the Marquess of Brabington and that you love him. You played that scene once on the boards in your acting days with touching pathos, as I recall.'

'And this is your idea of a joke! 'Tis monstrous!'

He shrugged. 'It's a wager. Brabington wants his flighty wife taken down a peg, but if ...'

'Wait! Do you mean this trick is with Brabington's *approval*?'

He smiled at her caressingly. 'Now, Harriet, *Harriet*, would I ask you to do it an I did not have my lord's approval?'

She looked at him doubtfully. 'Then why not come himself?'

'You must admit. It is a rather ... er ... delicate matter.'

Harriet sat frowning and thinking of the mountain of debt that was piling up over her head.

She thought of the security five hundred guineas could bring. She thought tenderly of the young wastrel she loved more than anyone in the world.

She did not for a moment think that the Marquess knew anything about it. She was sure Sir Guy was using her to get revenge. But on the other hand, Brabington could charm any woman, even an angry wife, and, as soon as it was over, she would confess she had only been play-acting for a joke.

As if reading her mind, he said, 'Part of the agreement would be that you must never admit it was a trick or tell how it came to be arranged.'

'But you said it was with Brabington's approval.'

'Exactly, but he still wishes it to remain a secret.'

Well, he was only confirming what she had guessed, that he was merely playing a vicious trick on the Brabingtons. But, oh! how she needed that money!

'But it will cause such a scandal,' protested Harriet, and people may call here and ask awkward questions.'

'I had thought of that,' he smiled. 'I have a house at Brighton you could use for a month until the heat dies down. Just think, Harriet, sea breezes, fashionable company, no rent to pay, no duns or creditors on your doorstep ... and *five hundred guineas.*'

Harriet chewed a fingernail and looked at the floor. She had played tricks on members of society before. One young lord had paid her handsomely once to turn up on his brother's doorstep, claiming to be the rightful wife. They were all mad, these society men. Too little to do and too much money. She had never had an affair with Brabington. He had escorted her to a couple of outings and to the theatre once, but his interest in her seemed to pall quickly. She had been very surprised when he had called to take her for a drive.

She had been halfway to being in love with him when he had dropped her so abruptly, and a little bit of that still rankled.

She thought of Harry Persalt, thought of the joy on his face when she told him they would be able to leave town

144

for a little.

'I'll do it,' she said suddenly. 'When?'

'In a little,' he smiled. 'I will let you know.'

Harriet was suddenly anxious for him to be gone before she changed her mind. The very air of the little room seemed to be filling with suffocating malice.

To her relief, he rose and made his bow.

Sir Guy Wayne stood smiling outside the villa, drawing on his dogskin gloves and breathing in the morning air of Islington. Far away across the fields, borne by the wind, tolled the deep, booming clang of the great bell of St Sepulchre's heralding another condemned man's road to the gallows.

He swung himself up into his phaeton and picked up the reins. He felt quite exhausted. He could not remember having worked so hard of a morning for quite a long while.

Annabelle was spared her husband's presence at the breakfast table and did not know whether to be glad or sorry.

She called at Lady Godolphin's to say farewell to her family as they set out for Hopeworth. To her surprise, she found her father and Squire Radford had agreed to stay on in Town. The way her father's shrewd little eyes kept fastening on her face made her uneasy. It was hard to feel like a mature married woman in front of a parent who so obviously still considered her a hoydenish schoolgirl.

She kissed her sisters and her mother goodbye, promised to visit the boys at their preparatory school in the King's Road, and waved a tearful farewell as the ancient Armitage coach with John Summers beaming on the box and the maid, Betty, beaming inside turned the corner of Hanover Square and disappeared.

When she returned to Conduit Street there was a new lady's maid, found by the enterprising Jensen, to interview.

She was called Holden, a wiry middle-aged woman with a stultifying air of gentility. But she seemed to combine briskness with deference and had brought beautiful examples of her skill with the needle.

Annabelle engaged her, and Holden said she was prepared to begin her duties at once. So that was that. Holden set about preparing my lady to receive afternoon callers, setting and arranging her blonde hair with such artistry that Annabelle realized Jensen had found a treasure.

She entertained various callers, the gentlemen she had danced with the night before, Lady Godolphin who was very welcome, and the Duchess of Allsbury who was not. Annabelle was just beginning to rejoice over two things – the first, that her husband had sent a message to say he would be escorting her to the opera that evening, and the second, Mr Wayne had not called. But as far as the latter was concerned, her joy was to be short-lived. For no sooner had the grim Duchess taken her leave than Sir Guy was introduced.

But again Annabelle found all her doubts melting under the pleasant warmth of his manner. He implied, without going quite so far as to say so, that he had drunk too much the previous evening. He made the story of his ducking in the pool so amusing that Annabelle found herself laughing and secretly admiring him for being such a good sport.

He did not stay above ten minutes, but asked her on leaving if he would have the pleasure of seeing her at any of the social engagements in town that evening. Annabelle hesitated slightly and then confessed that she would be at the opera. She found herself hoping he would not promptly say that he would be there too, for she felt if she did not spend some time alone with her husband, the difficulties of their marriage would never be resolved. But, almost as if he had read her thoughts, he spread his hands in a deprecatory movement and sighed that unfortunately he was otherwise engaged.

His manner towards her was amused as well as amusing; his pale eyes cool and mocking. Despite her better nature, Annabelle found herself beginning to flirt a little, for she was intrigued by his changes from hot to cold.

146

After he had left, she found herself thinking about him and wondering if he could possibly be used to make her infuriating husband jealous. But that would never do. She dismissed the thought almost as soon as it had been formed. Her duty was to convince her husband that the mention of Sylvester's name had been a mere slip of the tongue, nothing more.

Annabelle fretted over what to wear for the opera. Then she found that her experienced lady's maid had, of course, selected the right dress. It was a rather plain frock of amber satin shot with white and ornamented around the bosom and waist with a rich white silk trimming, called frost work. A long row of pearl buttons fastened the dress at the back. The white lace sleeves were very full and fastened about the middle of the arm by a broad band of 'letting in' lace. The gown ended in a demi-train.

Annabelle found herself wondering whether her lord would consider her over-extravagant if she ordered new gowns. The dresses Minerva had given her were very fine, but they *were* Minerva's, and it would be so pleasant to have brand new ones, all of her own.

To her surprise, Holden, the maid, came back with a heavy chest from which she proceeded to take out an amethyst tiara and matching necklace.

'How did you come by these, Holden?' she asked.

'From the master, my lady. My lord left the jewels with Jensen. They are the Brabington jewels.'

It says much for the new Annabelle's chastened state of mind that she did not fly over to the box to see what else was there. For the moment it was enough to accept the gift of the jewels as a token that he had forgiven her behaviour of the night before.

'But what about *his* behaviour?' thought Annabelle suddenly, as the maid carefully arranged the tiara on her blonde curls.

'What of Lady Coombes? What if *she* is at the opera, looking for a chance to tell Peter he has the best legs in London?'

She was so engrossed in this new worry that she was

half way down the stairs with Holden following her, carrying her cloak, her reticule and her fan, before Annabelle realized that, for once, she had forgotten to paint.

Her hand flew nervously to her face which felt all at once young, and, somehow, naked.

After all, going to the opera was every bit as terrifying as going to Almack's. The opera was a social function which entirely outclassed anything of the sort at Court after the retirement of poor, mad George III. There was no question of getting in by the mere payment of money. A committee of ladies supervised the issue of every ticket, and a man or a lady went to the opera or did not, depending on whether their social position was or was not considered worthy of that honour by the Lady Patronesses.

The performance did not matter in the least. One went to see the peerless Mr Brummell with his satellite Exquisites in Fop's Alley. The ladies of the grand tier were more anxious to gain his attention than that of the Prince Regent. The interest of the evening was not, 'How good is the production?' but rather, 'How well got up is Mr Brummell?'

The dandies displayed their graces with as much thought as the ladies – Mr George Damer, Lord Foley, Mr Henry Pierrepoint, Mr Wellesley Pole, Mr Charles Standish, Mr Drummond and Mr Lumley Skeffington.

She waited nervously at the door of the drawing room for her husband to make some comment on her appearance, but all he said was, 'I see you have the jewels,' and then motioned to Holden to help her mistress into the cloak.

On the road to the opera Annabelle said, 'Brabington, perhaps I could be advised ahead of time as to which social engagements we are to attend.'

'As you wish,' he replied indifferently.

There was a silence between them. And then he said casually, 'I had forgot. You had best employ the lightning talents of Madame Verné. We are to attend the Queen's

148

Drawing Room next week.'

'The Queen!' shrieked Annabelle. 'I will need a court dress.'

'Exactly. Jensen tells me you have a new lady's maid. Take her with you to the dressmaker.'

'Will you be going with me?'

'Of course.'

'And how long have you known this?'

'Some time. You must forgive me. I am afraid it slipped my memory.'

Annabelle tried to read his expression in the darkness of the carriage. All at once, she wanted to tell him that her forthcoming court appearance frightened her, that she felt nervous and unsure. She had a sudden longing for the vicarage, and for Minerva's quiet voice, telling her that everything would be all right. But Minerva was bucketing about on the high seas by now.

Annabelle did not think of Lord Sylvester at all.

The opera was a blaze of candlelight and jewels. It was a performance of Mozart's *Cosi Fan Tutte*, billed as an *opera buffa* in two acts.

As they ascended the staircase, the Marquess kept stopping to introduce her to various acquaintances. Lady Coombes' hard sophisticated face seemed to leap out of the crowd. She laid her gloved hand on the Marquess's arm, talking to him eagerly of friends and places that Annabelle did not know. At last, the Marquess murmured something about being late for the performance, and Lady Coombes flashed Annabelle a thin, hard smile and sank into a curtsey.

Looking out between the red curtains of the Marquess of Brabington's box, Annabelle found herself viewing a sea of jewels, bare shoulders, taffeta, feathers, lace, uniforms, quizzing glasses and curving top hats, all moving and glittering under the hot lights of thousands of candles.

She was lucky in that she had a relatively clear view of the stage. Some of the other boxes had their view nearly totally obscured by a chandelier full of lighted candles hung between them and the stage.

The short overture was soon over and the curtains drew back to plunge Annabelle into another world. Had she been an ardent music lover, had she known more of Mr Mozart's operas, and had she been more in the way of going to London performances, then she might have been appalled at the production and the difficulties of concentration.

Up in the galleries footmen, tradesmen and sailors whistled and howled and cracked nuts while the ladies of the night plied their trade, selling themselves for a shilling and a glass of rum.

In the main body of the audience the candlelight winked from quizzing glasses and opera glasses as society studied each other and ignored what was going on on the stage.

And it is doubtful if Mozart would have recognized parts of his opera. From time to time, his beautiful music was interrupted by one of the characters bursting into a well-known English popular song – wildly applauded by the audience – before returning to the theme of the opera.

But to Annabelle, it was magic. Eagerly she followed the complications of the plot, sympathizing with the sisters, Fiordiligi and Dorabella. Secretly she thought she would never forgive any man for the sort of trick the sister's fiancés played on them – pretending to be two other men to test their fidelity. But she sighed with pure happiness when the four lovers were at last reunited.

She turned a radiant face to the Marquess. 'Oh, *thank* you,' she said simply.

'I had more enjoyment, I confess, watching your face than the production,' he said. For a moment she caught a glimpse of the old warmth and affection in his face and a hand seemed to clutch her heart, followed by a yearning to keep him looking at her in just that way.

She fretted while he lingered, talking to various people on their road out of the opera house. Was it really necessary to spend so much time speaking to Lady Coombes?

At last they were in the carriage together, jogging through the streets, and Annabelle was glad to leave the

150

world of society behind. She chattered on enthusiastically about the opera and he smiled lazily and promised to take her as much as he could during the Season.

'But we are not going home!' exclaimed Annabelle, looking out of the window.

'I must beg you to forgive me again,' he said with no hint of apology in his voice. 'We are continuing a musical evening by going on to a *musicale* at Lord and Lady Brothers. They are friends of Sylvester and also of mine.'

'You are treating me like a child, Brabington,' said Annabelle sharply. 'I do not like to be dragged hither and thither without a by-your-leave.'

'All these invitations are in the card rack in the drawing room,' he replied equably. 'Although they come addressed to me, it is your privilege to reject those you do not wish to attend.'

Annabelle bit her lip, and then said in a milder voice, 'Perhaps I should have realized that, but I am not yet accustomed to the ways of society, and do not know yet as to how to go on.'

He took her hand and held it in a light clasp.

'I am a monster of thoughtlessness, am I not? You are so beautiful and so *mondaine*, my sweeting, that I forget you are new to the world. I shall behave myself in future.' He raised her hand and kissed it, and Annabelle experienced a suffocating feeling that was part pleasure, part pain,

'I am pleased you are wearing some of the jewels. What did you think of them?' he asked. 'The diamond tiara is rather fine. I thought you would have worn it.'

'I did not look at the rest,' said Annabelle. 'My new maid, Holden, selected these.'

'You did not look!' he echoed. Then he smiled. 'On second thought, her choice was wise.'

They rode on in a companionable silence. 'If only the evening could go on like this,' thought Annabelle. 'If only he does not make one of his lightning changes of mood.'

Annabelle was surprised to find her father and Squire Radford present. Her father gave her a hearty greeting as they took their seats for the *musicale*. A rather shrill soprano began to sing several arias. The vicar promptly fell asleep and snored loudly. Squire Radford nudged him and he came awake with a shout of, 'There he goes. After him boys!' which infuriated the singer and convulsed the company.

Annabelle was not aware of the length of the concert or of the strident tones of the diva. Her husband was holding her hand and she felt she would be content to sit like this for a very long time indeed.

Squire Radford looked at the couple's joined hands and nudged the vicar again. 'I'm not sleepin',' grumbled the vicar. The Squire pointed and the vicar looked at the clasped hands of the Brabingtons, a slow smile spreading over his ruddy face. 'Praise be, we can go home now, Jimmy, and leave this pesky city. All's well, heh!'

Annabelle drifted through the evening in a happy daze, her tall husband always at her side. There was no Lady Coombes and no Sir Guy Wayne.

Dawn was pearling the sky when they at last headed homewards. She put her head on his shoulder and closed her eyes contentedly, feeling the warmth of his body next to hers in the swaying coach, lulled by the rhythmic clip-clop of the horses' hooves over the cobbles.

With an arm around her waist he led her into the house in Conduit Street, and so they mounted the stairs. He stopped outside her bedroom door and took her very gently in his arms, feeling the way her body yielded against his and noticing the way she turned her lips up for his kiss.

'Not yet,' he said, half to himself. He bent his head and kissed her very softly on the lips.

'Goodnight,' he said huskily and turned away.

'Peter,' she whispered urgently, but either he did not hear or affected not to. She stayed for a few moments, a crease of worry between her eyes, looking down the blackness of the corridor, and then she slowly opened the door of her bedroom and went inside.

CHAPTER NINE

The next few days passed in a whirl of outings and parties, paying calls, and visiting Madame Verné so that a court dress could be made as quickly as possible.

The Marquess was now to be seen everywhere with his wife. He even came to Madame Verné's with her, and to the fashionable plumier, Carberry, since ladies to be presented at Court were obliged to wear at least seven plumes. Beneath the plumes, Annabelle was to wear on her head a garland of white roses resting upon a circlet of pearls. The finishing touches to her headdress were to be given by diamond buckles, a diamond comb, and tassels of white silk.

As the Court dress was built around her Annabelle began to wonder how any lady was expected to move in it. When the bodice of her dress was fitted on, an enormous hooped skirt, three ells long, was laced to her waist.

The skirt was made of waxed calico stretched upon whalebone. Over this skirt went a satin skirt, and over the satin skirt went one of tulle, ornamented with a large furbelow of silver lace.

A fourth and shorter skirt, also of tulle with silver spangles, ornamented with a garland of flowers, was turned up so that the garland surmounted the skirt crosswise. The openings of the tucks were ornamented with lace and surmounted with a large bouquet of flowers. The bottom of the white satin dress with its silver embroidery was turned up in loops and did not reach the bottom of the skirt, such being the fashionable etiquette, since only the royal princesses were allowed to wear skirts that were not turned up.

Madame Verné told Annabelle that one must try to wear *all* the jewels from one's jewel box about one's person.

153

The style seemed over-ornate and fussy to a girl as young as Annabelle who had grown up with the uncluttered, simple Grecian lines which were still very much in vogue.

She was also expected to carry a large bouquet of flowers.

But somehow the long and tedious fittings were fun, for the Marquess was always with her, telling her amusing stories, teasing her, and assuring her she would be the most beautiful lady at Court.

Although he kissed her lightly each night, he showed no signs of wanting any increased intimacy, and Annabelle found herself beginning to long to see passion flame in his eyes. He was *hers*, her husband. She wanted to feel secure. She did not want to have to worry about designing harpies like Lady Coombes luring him away.

As she finally stood being made ready by Holden for the Court Drawing Room, she could not help wondering if he still regarded her as a child. Her father had left for the country after the evening of the *musicale*, clapping her affectionately on the shoulder and congratulating her on 'becoming a woman at last'.

Annabelle sometimes wondered if the Marquess were waiting for some show of warmth on *her* side. She had considered several times in the past few days trying to explain away the use of Sylvester's name on her wedding night. But, on consideration, she decided that, on the one hand, she did not want to lie to him, and, on the other, she was sure the truth would be too shocking. She must, somehow, *show* him that he had all her love.

And that, thought Annabelle with surprise, was that! She loved him.

She did not just want him because he was her husband, her property. She wanted his love in return.

Perhaps she should tell him she loved him. Just like that. Before they left for the Queen's House.

But she dreaded the idea of rejection.

Feeling very strange and heavy in her Court dress and with nine white feathers bobbing on her head and a tremendous weight of jewels hung about her person, Annabelle was assisted down the stairs by her anxious maid and two footmen, despite her protests that she would have to manage on her own once she got there.

The Marquess was waiting for her at the foot of the stairs. He, too, was in full Court dress and Annabelle thought he had never looked more magnificent.

He was wearing a purple velvet coat ornamented with silver embroidery. His breeches were of fine silk edged with silver lace and he wore black shoes with diamond buckles. He had his dress sword with a jewelled hilt at his side and he carried his chapeau bras under his arm. His black hair was covered with a white wig and diamonds blazed all over his body.

He surveyed her in silence and then smiled. 'You look as if you are arising from a bouquet of flowers,' he said.

He leaned forwards and kissed her lightly on the nose. 'It's rather like leaning over a flower bed to kiss a maid at the cottage window,' he laughed.

'As you have no doubt done many times, sir,' said Annabelle.

'If I have, I forget. I can see only you,' he replied, his eyes serious.

Annabelle tried to say she loved him, but the servants were waiting and somehow the words caught in her throat.

The Queen's House, the former residence of the Duke of Buckingham, stood at the end of the Mall. Although they had to wait in a long line of carriages, there was plenty to look at. All the carriages were glittering with new varnish, new hammer cloths, and with two or three liveried footmen on the back. The horses, all in prime condition, moved proudly under heavy emblazoned harness.

Trumpets were sounding and the Park and Tower guns were firing.

The Mall was lined by ranks of cavalry in scarlet, with their bright helmets and jet black horses, their gloves of white buckskin stiffened so that the cuffs reached half way up the elbow.

155

The waiting was not over after the palace, or the Queen's House as it was called, was reached.

Hundreds were arriving at the same time as Annabelle and the Marquess, and hundreds who had already paid their respects were trying to get away.

At the first landing of the entrance hall the staircase branched off into two arms, one arm being used for those going up, and the other for those going down. Both staircases seemed made up of waving columns of plumes. Some were sky blue, some were tinged with red. There was violet, yellow, and shades of green. In the main, the plumes were snow-white like those worn by Annabelle. Then there were jewels of every description, flashing and winking, catching fire and flame as the ladies twisted this way and that on the staircase to manoeuvre their hoops.

The men seemed as if they were trying to outshine the ladies in magnificence. One man looked like a jewellers' display case, he had so many gems laid out on his portly person.

The Exquisites flocked about, dressed in the ultra-pitch of fashion, each collared like the leader of a four-horse team, pinched in the middle like an hourglass, with a neck as long as a goose and a cravat as ample as a tablecloth. Quite a number of the men were rouged, and one elderly gentleman even wore patches. Some of the younger, more willowy Pinks of the Ton had tinged the palms of their hands with vermilion and had whitened the backs with enamel.

A young Merveilleux caused Annabelle to stare. He was so perfumed and wigged and corsetted and painted that she wondered if anything could be left of the original man when he was dismantled by his valet for the night.

But at least, Annabelle thought, there was one thing to be said for this preposterous style of dress as far as the female sex was concerned – at least one could distinguish the ladies.

This was not always the case with the usual mode of evening gown. One theatre tried to keep the Fashionable Impure from its doors by appointing two door-keepers for

156

the purpose.

But this had to be stopped early in the evening since the two men had nearly conveyed a couple of ladies of very high degree to the watch-house. How could one tell the Cyprians from the ladies of quality when both were dressed in a state of semi-nudity?

There was also a refreshing return of formal manners. In many cases, brutal manners towards the female had taken the place of the last century's ceremonious demeanour and good breeding.

After three-quarters of an hour of swaying backwards and forwards in the press from step to step, Annabelle at last found herself in the presence of Queen Charlotte.

King George, of course, was not present, and never would be again. It was feared his madness showed no sign of abating.

His madness had been ignored as long as possible but when he at last descended from his carriage and shook hands heartily with the branches of a tree, under the impression that he was paying his respects to the King of Prussia, it was decided his malady had gone too far. Lord Sheffield reported that the King could still be quite cheerful. 'The King's illness is not melancholy or mischievous,' he reported. 'At times it is rather gay. He fancies London is drowned and orders his yacht to go there. In one of his soliloquies, he said, "I hate nobody, why should anyone hate me?" Recollecting a little, he added, "I beg pardon, I do hate the Marquis of Buckingham."'

Annabelle had heard many stories of this little martinet Queen who ruled her court in the stiff and formal manner of the German courts.

Annabelle was led forwards and made her curtsey to the Queen and to the royal princesses. Queen Charlotte looked sourly at her, took snuff, said gruffly to the Marquess, 'How d'ye do?' and then turned her attention to the next in line.

Annabelle was glad to escape. But another three-quarters of an hour passed before they could get down the

157

stairs, another hour waiting for their carriage, and an hour and a half to get down the Mall.

'I shall be glad to get home,' yawned Annabelle. 'I want to *slouch*. I feel as if I am on show in a flowered cage.'

'We shall have a simple supper first,' said the Marquess. 'All that confounded bowing and scraping gives me an appetite.'

'The 'simple supper' turned out to consist of soup, fish, fricassée of chicken, cutlets, venison, veal, hare, vegetables of all kinds, tart, melon, pineapple, grapes, peaches and nectarines.

They were waited on by six servants, a butler and a gentleman-in-waiting. The gentleman-in-waiting was an indispensable part of every gentleman's retinue. At house parties, you were expected to bring your gentleman-in-waiting to stand behind your chair during dinner, ready to shovel you off the floor when you fell down drunk.

Annabelle had quickly learned to consume quite a large quantity of wine without feeling dizzy. Champagne, she had also quickly learned, was 'vulgar'. Claret went with the meat and tokay with the pudding. Hock, sherry and port or port-and-water could be served throughout the meal, although Brummell kept trying to insist that port – 'a hot, intoxicating liquor so much drunk by the lower orders' – should wait for the cheese.

Relaxed and happy, Annabelle began to amuse the Marquess with stories of her home life, of her frequent feuds with Deirdre, and how Minerva would always be called in to be the peacemaker.

'You miss your sister, do you not?' he asked.

'Oh, yes,' said Annabelle. 'I do wish she could see me in my Court dress.'

'I thought, my love, at one time that you were jealous of Minerva. That you wanted the ... er ... things that she had.'

'I had a silly bout of jealousy,' said Annabelle with lowered eyes and lowered voice. 'But that is gone.'

There was a silence. The candle flame burned clear and bright. The servants had retired. The fire crackled and hissed on the hearth.

'And Sylvester?' he asked softly.

'I had not yet grown up,' replied Annabelle, praying that he would understand.

'And now that you have?'

She raised her eyes to his, anxious, pleading. She wanted to say, 'Now, I love you as a woman should love a man.' But the words would not come. Suppose he laughed at her?

He gave a little sigh and began to talk of their plans for the morrow. He had military duties to attend to, he said, but he would be free in the evening to squire her to the opera.

Annabelle answered in monosyllables, her eyes fixed on her plate, cursing herself for her lack of courage, knowing that the moment to say something had passed.

She suddenly felt infinitely weary and infinitely young and helpless.

The days of this non-marriage seemed to stretch in front of her endlessly, days when she would worry and watch for the time when he would decide to console himself with another woman.

At last, he suggested that they retire. She was still wearing her finery and he courteously helped her to mount the stairs to her room.

She waited with downcast eyes for his usual brief goodnight embrace but he surprised her by holding open the door to her bedroom and following her inside.

Holden, who had been asleep beside the fire with some sewing on her lap, leapt to her feet.

'You may leave us, Holden,' said the Marquess, and Annabelle stood stiffly and awkwardly in the centre of the room until the maid had left.

'I am very afraid, Peter,' said Annabelle, 'and I do not know what I should do.'

The Marquess of Brabington moved towards her.

'Come, my sweeting,' he said, 'and let me show you.'

It had all been remarkably easy, thought Annabelle, some time later, as she lay with her head pillowed on his naked chest, listening to the steady beating of his heart.

An all-consuming passion had swept her along, teaching her to respond to him, casting out fear.

She stirred lazily in his arms and he whispered, 'Not asleep? I will love you again, if you are not careful.'

She laughed and turned against him and he pulled her naked body tightly against his own, his hands stroking and caressing her back and buttocks, until he heard her breathing quickening and felt her lips desperately seeking his own.

He made love to her very slowly this time, letting his hands and lips wander and trace patterns on her body, until she suddenly leapt alive like a wild animal, raking his back with her nails, begging and pleading and making odd little noises until he took her again.

And so they passed the night and the morning, buried in each other, sleeping and waking, and waking each time to find the lovemaking had become more intense.

Then finally Annabelle awoke, and he was gone. She felt langourously exhausted, placidly happy.

Until it hit her like a thunderclap. She had not said she loved him.

And he – he had not said he loved her either!

It should have been the happiest day of Annabelle's life. It proved to be the most disastrous.

She sent word to Jensen that she would not be receiving callers. She planned to spend a leisurely afternoon, reading a little, writing to Minerva, and then devote the early part of the evening to preparing for the opera.

She was seated at a little escritoire in the gloomy drawing room, trying to find words to tell Minerva of all the newfound happiness in her marriage. Mrs Armitage had given her an address in Naples to which to write.

She looked up in surprise as Jensen entered to tell her that there was a ... hem ... person demanding audience.

'A person, Jensen?'

'An extremely fashionable lady, but, I would venture to assess, more *demi* than *mondaine*.'

'Then send her about her business, Jensen.'

'The person appears to be in extreme distress, my lady, and said you would be anxious to see her although her name might mean nothing to you.'

'Where have you put her?'

'She is seated in the hall, my lady. She came without a maid,' answered Jensen with a sniff, as if this last piece of intelligence confirmed his opinion of the lady's character.

'Well, I will just look into the hall,' sighed Annabelle rising, 'and if it is someone I have never seen before, you may send her away.'

'Very good, my lady.'

The butler stood aside, holding open the door. Annabelle peeped around it, and then froze. 'Went as white as the lace at her throat,' as Jensen was to tell the servants' hall later.

'I will see her,' said Annabelle in a low voice. 'But answer immediately, should I ring the bell.'

She went and sat down, her hands clasped in her lap, her back very straight.

'Miss Harriet Evans,' announced Jensen lugubriously.

Both women surveyed each other curiously.

Annabelle had recognized her husband's fair partner from the Park.

Part of Annabelle's mind registered again with some surprise the unerring sense of social position that certain upper servants had. She herself would have thought Harriet Evans was a highly respectable lady.

'Please sit down, Miss Evans,' said Annabelle, 'and state your business.'

Harriet sat down demurely and raised her fine eyes to Annabelle's face. 'My lady,' she said in a low, throbbing voice, 'it breaks my heart to come here. But I am in sore distress and perhaps you should know the manner of man to whom you are married.'

'That is enough,' said Annabelle sharply. 'We do not

161

discuss our husband.'

'Not even when I am carrying his child?' said Harriet.

Annabelle's hand fluttered up to her throat. 'You had better explain,' she said in a dazed way.

'Before he was married, I was in his lordship's keeping, you understand, my lady. I was deeply in love. I am not a courtesan by nature. He showed all signs of being equally in love with me. I found I was pregnant and went to him for help. You have no doubt seen advertisements in the newspapers, my lady, put there by people who offer to relieve us of this kind of embarrassment.'

Annabelle shook her head dumbly.

'In short, I am speaking of an abortion. My lord begged me not to do it. He said he would look after me and the child. He said the child was a result of our love. He did not offer marriage, my lady, but somehow I assumed ...'

Harriet fumbled in her reticule, drew out a wisp of handkerchief, and dabbed at her eyes, while Annabelle sat rigidly watching her. 'The next thing I knew,' said Harriet in a stifled voice, 'was that he was married. I ... I thought of killing myself. But I do love him so, and ... and there is my unborn child to think of. It would be murder!'

Annabelle tried to think clearly. It could not be true! And yet the woman seemed to be in genuine distress. Peter had been seen driving her in the Park on the day after his wedding. All men of the Marquess's age had had some sort of liaison before their marriage. So her mind raced on and on, looking for an escape.

'What do you want me to do?' asked Annabelle desperately. 'I am very sorry for you Miss Evans. If it is money you wish ...?'

'No!' cried Harriet, 'as God is my judge.' And she turned her fine eyes up to the ceiling.

And all in that moment, Annabelle was forcibly reminded of Lady Godolphin confronting Colonel Brian. She took a deep breath.

'Look here, Miss Evans,' she said quietly. 'I do not know why you came here. I feel, somehow, that you are not telling the truth. My husband would never have

162

behaved in such a way.'

Harriet kept her handkerchief to her eyes while she thought busily.

Then she dropped the handkerchief, and got to her feet and looked down at Annabelle, her eyes alight with laughter.

'The trick has not worked, I see,' she smiled.

'Trick?'

'Oh, it was an idea of Peter's to see how much you loved him. He thought it would test your fidelity. I used to be an actress, my lady, but obviously I am not as good as I thought I was.'

Annabelle walked over to the fireplace and tugged the bell rope so ferociously that it came away in her hand.

'Jensen,' she said as the butler's curious face appeared at the door. 'Show this person out, and she is not to be admitted again.'

She turned her back on Harriet and stood looking into the fireplace.

Harriet made her way thoughtfully back to Islington. As she paid off the hack, she was not surprised to find Sir Guy Wayne lounging on the doorstep.

'Come in,' she said curtly, drawing off her gloves. He followed her into the cluttered parlour.

'I did as you requested,' said Harriet in a flat voice. 'She did not believe me. But when I told her it had been set up by her husband in order to test her fidelity, oh, she believed that.'

'You are sure?'

'Quite sure, and I tell you, Sir Guy, *that* caused her more hurt than had she believed the other.'

'Good,' he commented, drawing out a bag of guineas. 'You have earned your fee. I trust you are prepared to leave for Brighton today.'

Harriet took the money and then looked at him doubtfully. 'I fear you will find you have wasted your money, sir. She will simply confront Brabington with the matter when he arrives home, he will deny it, and that will be the end of it.'

'I am gambling that she will not,' smiled Sir Guy. 'I have never found my observation of human nature to be at fault. I have picked up rumours that the fair Marchioness was much smitten with Lord Sylvester Comfrey and merely married Brabington so as to outdo her sister. That, I feel sure, is why he flaunted you in the Park. Had the wedding night been one of bliss, then he would not have done such a thing.

'He did it to revenge himself on her. They are now in love and lately. That too I have observed. But this new love is a painfully fragile thing. She will remember his behaviour on the first few days after the marriage, and, as for him, he will remember hers. So she will be prepared to believe the worst. An I am not mistaken, she will simply turn cold and indifferent and will look around for a means to revenge herself on him. And I, my dear Harriet, will be at hand to supply her with the means. Then how can his lordship call me out when the young wife comes to my arms so willingly?'

Harriet shuddered. She wanted to fling the money in his face. But she needed it so badly. And she was sure he was mistaken. The Brabingtons were probably now in each other's arms and the whole thing would have been already forgotten.

Annabelle went automatically through the rest of the day, numb and stiff and hurt.

Perhaps if she had not seen *Cosi Fan Tutte* she would not have believed her husband would go to such lengths. But she had not seen Harriet with Sir Guy. She had only seen her with the Marquess. She thought of his cruel and erratic behaviour after her wedding night. She had put it down to a result of her use of Lord Sylvester's name. Now she began to see his actions as those of a heartless aristocrat, hell-bent on making fun at the expense of others.

By the time the Marquess arrived to take his wife to the opera, she felt completely indifferent to him. Never in her whole life had anyone treated Annabelle so cruelly. She answered all his compliments with a shrug and sat in rigid silence during the opera.

On the road home, he at last burst out with, 'What on earth is up with you, Annabelle?'

'You forget,' she said icily, 'I am to be trained in the conventions. You are to call me my lady at all times and I shall call you Brabington.'

'Did last night mean nothing to you?' he demanded furiously.

'I would rather forget about last night, sirrah!'

'And why, I wonder? Did you realize too late the wrong man held you in his arms?'

'If that is how you care to see it.'

He seemed to loom over her in the coach as he half rose from his seat, his bulk large and threatening.

She shrank back and he muttered an exclamation of disgust and rapped on the roof with his stick. As the coach rumbled to a halt he leapt out without waiting for the footmen to let down the steps.

'Where are you going?' shouted Annabelle. 'To Lady Coombes?'

'Why not?' he shouted back, striding off into the night.

A footman sprang down and shut the door. The carriage rumbled forwards and Annabelle sat fighting back tears.

There would have been one great flaw in Sir Guy Wayne's assessment of human nature if the couple had said they loved each other. But that was what rankled in each bosom, and that was what made each so ready to believe the worst of each other. Both Annabelle and her husband felt they had wasted all their tenderest love and passion on a frivolous, unworthy object.

Now all Annabelle wanted to do was to get away, away from this man who did not love her, to escape before he could torment her further.

All at once she decided to go home to Hopeworth. She would immerse herself in parish duties. But a saner side of her mind told her to have a good night's sleep and perhaps things would seem not so bad in the morning.

But in the morning, two things happened. A letter

arrived telling her curtly that she was refused vouchers to Almack's.

Annabelle was young and inexperienced enough to feel the social slight more than most. What cut most deep was that her husband had taken no steps to ensure her acceptance.

And then her cousins, Josephine and Emily Armitage, arrived. They had received their invitations and were in *alt.* They were carefully courteous to Annabelle, for, after all, she was now a marchioness, but they could not refrain from several silly and jealous remarks and the sisters finally seemed to Annabelle to epitomize all that was worst in London society, vain and silly and cruel.

After they had left she called Jensen and told him the travelling carriage was to be prepared to take her to Hopeworth. She then called him back and told him that she was ordering him not to tell the Marquess of Miss Evans' visit. Annabelle was determined that her husband should not realize how much he had hurt her.

She ordered Holden to pack her trunks and warned the maid she would be expected to put up at a country vicarage in more uncomfortable surroundings than she had been used to.

But Holden had worked for society for a long time and was used to the vagaries of the quality. She judged, rightly, that her master and mistress had had a quarrel, but she was sure it would soon be put to rights, and so resigned herself to rusticating in the country for a little.

She looked startled when Annabelle said that she would not be taking any of the Brabington jewels. They were to be left in her husband's room.

Then she sat down to write the Marquess a letter. She told him that she could not bear to live under the same roof any more and wished for a separation.

Coldly and efficiently she went about the preparations for the journey, her face hard and set.

The day was sunny and warm. The streets of London seemed to be thronged with happy carefree people as she slumped in the corner of the travelling carriage, looking out at them with dull eyes.

Before, God had been in his Heaven and everything had been very much all right with the world. Now Annabelle began to be haunted by the Old Testament God of vengeance, and, by the time her weary journey home was over, she was convinced that divine punishment had been visited on her for her jealousy of Minerva and for her wicked plans to seduce her brother-in-law.

A schoolgirl had left Hopeworth vicarage such a short time ago. It was a cold and rigid woman who arrived home.

Mrs Armitage attributed the change to Annabelle's high marriage and was duly impressed. Even the sharp-eyed Deirdre simply thought that Annabelle had become very high in the instep and failed to see the suffering which lurked under the cold and fashionable exterior.

Holden good-naturedly resigned herself to accepting quarters in a small attic room and cheerfully began to advise the Armitage sisters on dress and manners. A governess had not yet been found for them and so Mrs Armitage was delighted to have this unexpected mentor for the girls.

The vicar did not arrive back till late evening. Mrs Armitage had said he was about his duties, but it turned out he had spent an unsuccessful day's fishing.

He listened carefully to Annabelle's explanation for her homecoming. She said the Marquess was too taken up with military duties to escort her throughout the Season, and that since she missed her home she had thought it would be a good opportunity to pay them a visit.

The vicar was sharp set and did not want to think about anything but food. But as he pushed his plate away at the end of the meal, he thoughtfully picked his teeth and studied Annabelle's calm face.

He seemed to finally come to some conclusion, for, as Annabelle was explaining that she thought she would pay some calls on the morrow, he said, 'Don't make any plans, Bella. I will talk to you in the morning.'

Annabelle looked at him sharply, but his ruddy face

seemed quite bland as he poured his sixth glass of port with steady concentration.

She spent a restless, sleepless night, waking up at dawn in a sweat after a particularly vile dream in which she was standing at the altar at St George's, Hanover Square, holding the train of Lady Coombes' wedding gown, and Lady Coombes was marrying the Marquess of Brabington.

The morning dragged on. She tried to keep away from her sisters who were too full of questions about the glories of fashionable London.

Her father appeared before her like a stout jack-in-the-box. He looked at her carefully, at her white face and sad eyes.

'Get your bonnet, Bella,' he said roughly. 'We're going to pay a call.'

CHAPTER TEN

Annabelle sat beside her father in his open carriage, only vaguely aware of the warmth of the sun and the glory of the golden day.

The vicar swung round in front of Squire Radford's cottage *ornée* and helped Annabelle to alight.

The Squire's soft-footed Indian servant said his master was in the garden and led them there.

The Squire was amazed to see Annabelle, his eyes darting from her face to the vicar's.

He waited until they were all seated at a round table under the gently moving leaves of a sycamore tree. The Indian servant brought madeira for the vicar and lemonade for Annabelle and departed, leaving the silent company studying each other.

A little brook at the foot of the garden chattered over the pebbles on its way to join the River Blyne. Far away a dog barked and the hedges and trees were full of birdsong.

But winter was present in Annabelle's face.

'This is very pleasant,' said Squire Radford when his servant had left. 'I am surprised to find you in the country, my lady, with the Season only just begun. But you are welcome, very welcome. And Charles, too. Is there any special reason for your call, my dear Charles?'

'Yes,' said the vicar curtly. 'Her.' He jerked his head in Annabelle's direction.

'Dear me!' He turned to Annabelle sympathetically. 'You are in trouble, my dear?'

'No,' said Annabelle.

'Yes,' said the vicar of St Charles and St Jude.

'I am here because my husband is engaged in military duties,' said Annabelle in a high voice, unlike her own.

'They've quarrelled,' interrupted the vicar, 'and Bella's breaking her heart.'

Annabelle looked at her father haughtily and then her face seemed to break apart until she bent her head and burst into noisy tears.

The Squire made helpless little sounds of distress, but the vicar said callously, 'Leave her be, Jimmy, or we'll never get to the bottom of this.'

They waited until Annabelle had cried herself out and had blown her nose.

'I'm sorry,' she whispered.

'Very well,' said her father bracingly. 'Out with it. The whole story. Start from the beginning about how you was in love with Sylvester.'

'Oh, father,' wailed Annabelle, 'if you knew *that*, how could you let me make such a fool of myself?'

'I'm still waiting to hear how much of a fool you've been,' said the vicar drily. 'See here, Jimmy, this madeira's prime stuff.'

'Really Charles,' protested the Squire, and turning to Annabelle, 'Go on, my dear, we are only here to help you.'

Annabelle opened her mouth and began to talk.

She talked and talked while the sun climbed higher in the sky and the birds fell silent. She told them everything, of her jealousy of Minerva, of her falling in love with her husband, of the trick he had played on her.

'By Gad!' cried the vicar angrily. The Squire saw his friend was about to burst out and tell Annabelle that they had told her husband to behave wickedly, so he rose quickly and helped Annabelle to her feet. 'You must leave us to discuss this,' he said gently. 'Go to my library and have a little rest. You will find it has all been a dreadful mistake. Go now.'

Annabelle felt so weary after her confession that she felt she could sleep for days. She did not see what she or anyone else could do to mend matters, but she obeyed the Squire and left them to their discussion.

'He went too far,' began the vicar wrathfully.

'My dear Charles, pray calm yourself,' said Squire Radford. 'I am persuaded the Marquess had no hand in this so-called trick.

170

'You are not thinking coolly. Now, we will go over Annabelle's story again, bit by bit.' They turned it this way and that; Annabelle had told them about everyone she had met and about the two humiliations of Sir Guy Wayne.

'Now don't you think,' mused the Squire, half closing his eyes against the sun and putting the tips of his fingers together, 'that either Sir Guy or Lady Coombes would have more of an interest in tricking Annabelle? It must be someone who knew the marriage very well, else why would they not think that the Brabingtons would confront each other. Annabelle did not even tell Brabington that the woman had called. I think he should be told that.'

'Very well,' said the vicar, 'we'll write to him.'

The squire sighed and looked around his sunny garden. 'No,' he said reluctantly, 'we must go, Charles. Today.'

'A pox on all daughters,' grumbled the vicar, heaving himself out of his chair. 'They're worse than foxes any day. Now foxes at least give a man some sport.'

'Well,' smiled the Squire, 'this is in the nature of a hunt. Come Charles. There is no need to tell Annabelle our plans.'

But the pair met with a setback as soon as they arrived at Conduit Street. The Marquess had already departed for his estates in the country and had left no word when he would be returning.

'There you are,' said the vicar with gloomy satisfaction, 'that shows he ain't got his eye on any lightskirt. Mind you, 'tis no wonder they quarrelled. A saint would quarrel faced with the mausoleum atmosphere of this house. Did you ever seen anything so cold and gloomy?'

'Where to now?' asked the Squire.

'Lady Coombes,' said the vicar. 'I have her direction.'

Lady Coombes was startled to receive a call from the vicar of St Charles and St Jude but concealed her surprise under her usual haughty manner.

But she could not conceal her surprise or anger when

this clergyman asked her abruptly, 'D'ye know a lightskirt called Harriet Evans?'

'Really sir,' said Lady Coombes. 'You should ask your son-in-law. He was once *épris* in that direction.'

'Were you?' demanded the vicar, studying her closely. 'Were you taken with Brabington?'

She flushed to the roots of her hair, then closed her mouth like a steel trap, and called two footmen to eject her unwelcome visitors at the double.

'Now what?' said the vicar crossly. 'That one's mean enough for anything.'

'She might consider flirting with another woman's husband,' said the Squire, 'but she is too proud to approach a Cyprian for any reason.'

'So?'

'So, I think we pay a call on Miss Evans.'

But Miss Evans was gone from London, said the grumpy housemaid, a piece of news which depressed the hunters no end, their first thought being that the Marquess had taken his Fancy to the country.

But the housemaid could not resist adding, 'But my lips are sealed.'

'So are mine,' said the vicar. 'Sealed with dust. So let's all repair to the Barley Mow and see if we can remedy the defect. It's a while since I've had a pretty wench on my arm.'

'Oh, sir,' giggled the housemaid, tossing her huge mob cap so that it fell over her eyes. 'And you a vicar!'

'Which means you'll be safe with me,' said the vicar, leering awfully. 'Come along. I ain't going to ask you to speak.'

Giggling shrilly, the housemaid allowed herself to be propelled through the doors of the Barley Mow, and after eight glasses of gin-and-hot winked at the vicar, and said she could tell him a thing or two.

'No, you couldn't,' said the vicar cheerfully. 'I'll tell *you* something, my gel, you ain't got one secret in that pretty cockloft o' yours.'

'I 'ave so.'

'Go on,' said the vicar with a yawn. 'Prove it.'

'You won't tell a soul?'

'My word as a man of God,' said the vicar piously. ' "Stolen waters are sweet, and bread eaten in secret is pleasant." Proverbs, Chapter 9, Verse 17.'

'Not apt,' muttered the Squire.

'Well,' said the maid, 'I'm that worrit with duns on the doorstep and t'ain't fair, them being in Brighton and leaving me to cope though they paid my wages.'

'Them?' asked the vicar softly.

'My mistress and her gentleman friend, Mr Persalt. Some rich friend let them 'ave his villa at Brighton.'

'On the Marine Parade?' asked the vicar with seeming indifference.

'Naw, nothing so grand for the likes o' them. Some square it is. James Square, number nine, that's it.'

The vicar, having got what he came for, would have left immediately. But Squire Radford was more soft-hearted and insisted that they stayed for at least two more rounds of drinks.

'Brighton,' groaned the vicar. 'Let's rack up for the night and set out tomorrow, Jimmy. I'm mortal tired.'

But the Squire was tougher than his frail build suggested. 'Have you considered,' he said, 'that if we do not solve this problem quickly, Brabington may rejoin his regiment, and Annabelle may soon be a widow of the war?'

'Oh, whoresons of lovers. Why do you plague me?' cried the vicar, waving his fists at the sky. 'Very well, Jimmy. Let's away.'

They took the stage and arrived in Brighton very late in the evening. Even the Squire decided that they should begin their investigations at first light.

The vicar was clever enough to ask for an audience with Mrs Persalt the following morning, since his memory told him that tarts removed from their customary milieu were apt to appear as married woman as soon as they got out of town.

Mrs Persalt was pleased to see the vicar. She assumed

173

he had come from a local church to ask for funds and it gave her a warm feeling of respectability.

The vicar cunningly fostered this idea until he saw a good bottle of port being produced. He held his fire until he had downed one glass in a gulp and filled up another.

'Well, Miss Evans,' he said. 'You've done pretty well for yourself.'

Harriet's face blanched.

'You wouldn't want all them duns and creditors to know your direction, now would you?' pursued the vicar, his little eyes boring into her. 'So you be a good girl and tell me who set you up to that trick you played on the Marchioness of Brabington?'

'No one set me up,' said Harriet. 'It was Brabington himself. Who *are* you?'

'I am the Marchioness of Brabington's father and the Marquess of Brabington's father-in-law and I take leave to tell you, madam, that you have been telling a monstrous pack o' lies. What you did was shameless. Do you know that my daughter has separated from her husband, believing every vile word you said?'

'I needed the money,' said Harriet, beginning to cry. 'I was sure it would all be sorted out and they would talk to each other about it.'

'Who paid you to do this thing?' put in the Squire, his voice soft and gentle.

Harriet turned away from the bullying vicar and whimpered to the Squire, 'It was Sir Guy Wayne. He thought that I had had a liaison at one time with Brabington, but I swear that is not true. But, you see, Brabington took me driving in the Park the day after he was wed, and his bride saw us, so naturally she believed ...'

'So much for our plots,' muttered the vicar.

'You see,' went on Harriet desperately, 'Sir Guy guessed aright after all. He said he was a student of human nature. He told me that Brabington might come looking for me, and he offered me this house in Brighton for a month. It was too tempting. I had to get away. How

174

did you find me?'

'Never mind,' said the vicar. 'My daughter told the servants not to tell Brabington of your visit, so you were lucky in that respect.

'Now, see here, I don't like to cause a pretty lady distress,' went on the vicar, shooting an appreciative look at her ankles, 'so you just be a good girl and tell me where to find Sir Guy.'

'He will take revenge on me!'

'By the time I have finished with him,' said the Reverend Charles Armitage, 'he won't be fit to take revenge on anyone.'

'He had lodgings in St James's Street, 158 St James's Street.'

'Come along, Jimmy,' said the vicar. 'There's work to do.'

Squire Radford thought he had never seen his friend look so grim.

But when a weary Squire Radford and the vicar called at Sir Guy's lodgings, it was to find he had left town.

They repaired to a coffee house to mull over the matter.

'Do you think perhaps he has fled the country?' asked the Squire.

'Not he,' said the vicar roundly. 'Why should he? He doesn't know we have found anything.'

'It seems terrible to be so inactive after all our efforts,' sighed the Squire.

'Well, there's one thing we can do,' said the vicar, draining his glass.

'Which is?'

'Gossip. Come on. We're going to every club, every gaming house, every coffee house and every tattletale's drawing room in the whole of London. He won't have a shred o' reputation by the time I've finished with him.'

To the Squire it seemed as if his burly friend was indefatigable. He drank and talked and drank and talked from Grosvenor Square to St James's Square until society was alive with the gossip about the perfidy of Sir Guy.

At the end of three days, the little Squire's energy was beginning to flag. They were sitting in the Green Saloon at Lady Godolphin's, being regaled by that lady with tea and cakes. For once in his life, the vicar shuddered at the idea of anything stronger.

'You have written to Brabington, o'course,' said Lady Godolphin, who had heard the whole story blow by blow.

'No, I haven't,' cried the vicar, striking his brow.

'Follicles!' said Lady Godolphin. 'Write now and one of my men will ride direct to the country with your letter.'

The vicar scribbled away busily, crossing and recrossing several sheets until he was satisfied with the result. Then he sanded and sealed it and handed it to a servant.

'Now,' he said, 'all we've got to do is find the villain.'

'Perhaps he's gone after Annabelle,' said Lady Godolphin. 'That one always preys on young married gels.'

'Oh, my head,' groaned the vicar. 'Of course he has. What else would he do. I'm an idiot!'

'No, you ain't,' said Lady Godolphin warmly. 'You're a good patter familiar that's what you are. Annabelle should be grateful to you.'

But she spoke to the empty air, for the vicar had charged from the room with the Squire scuttling after him.

Two days before this, Annabelle had been surprised when Betty came into her bedroom and announced there was a caller for her.

'Ever such a fine gentleman, my lady,' said Betty.

'It's not ...? No, of course it can't be,' said Annabelle. How silly to hope it might be her husband.

She never wanted to see him again – or did she? Her mind had been in a turmoil since her father had left. She did not know he had travelled to London, since he had left word he had gone to a horse fair in the next county, and so she was rather disappointed to think that her father had

176

extracted her painful story from her and then had not troubled himself any further about it.

She was plagued with dreams of the Marquess and sometimes tormented with feelings of guilt. Perhaps she had acted too hastily. She could have told him. At least she could have given him a chance to explain. She had written letter after letter to him but had always ended up by tearing them in shreds.

Annabelle went slowly down and opened the drawing room door.

Sir Guy Wayne rose and came to meet her.

'Lady Annabelle,' he said in an unctuous voice. 'I heard of your separation from your husband. Servants *will* talk.

'I felt I must let you know that you had at least one friend in the *beau monde*.'

Servants did indeed talk as Sir Guy had found out to his advantage, although it had cost him quite a bit of money to bribe the information out of the Brabington household.

'You are very kind, Sir Guy, but I am quite happy. I am afraid we cannot put you up. We do not have any spare rooms.'

'I am billeted at the local inn,' he smiled. 'London is very flat and stale without your presence.'

'I would rather not talk about my husband, Sir Guy,' said Annabelle. 'We are not separated. He has military matters to attend to and I took this opportunity to see my family.'

'I heard your vouchers at Almack's had been refused,' he said sympathetically. 'Ah, if only I had known.'

'It does not matter,' said Annabelle, thinking bitterly, was there *anything* Sir Guy did not know? She pictured her shame being spread about London and felt a wave of pain.

'It is a beautiful day,' he said. 'I am unfamiliar with these parts and wondered if you would care to take the air with me?'

Annabelle hesitated. But she was touched by his loyalty. She said she would fetch her bonnet.

And so they walked and talked. Mrs Armitage was delighted to have such a fashionable visitor and Sir Guy

177

ate his dinners at the vicarage.

The little girls liked him with the exception of Deirdre who shuddered aristically and said he reminded her of a fish.

'He is not at all fishlike,' protested Annabelle. He is very much a gentleman.'

'It's his eyes,' said Deirdre. 'Flat and somehow watchful. They make me think of cold, bloodless things.'

Sir Guy showed no signs of behaving in too warm a manner and Annabelle began to enjoy his company. Her heart still ached for her husband but Sir Guy would apologetically drop little snippets about the Marquess's scandalous career and then say in confusion, 'I am sorry. I do keep forgetting you are married to him,' in such a natural and contrite way that Annabelle was quite convinced he spoke the truth.

The Marquess of Brabington began to seem more and more like a cruel and heartless rake who broke hearts as regularly as Lord Alvanley ate apricot tart.

It seemed the most natural thing in the world that he should attend church service with them on Sunday. Mr Pettifor, the vicar's overworked curate, was officiating in his master's absence.

It was a day of sun and showers with great ragged black and gray clouds tearing across a pale blue sky.

The girls' skirts fluttered in the warm wind as Annabelle, Sir Guy and Mrs Armitage led the family procession to church.

It was April. Bluebells carpeted the woods on either side of the road. The hornbeam was in flower and daffodils were blowing among the tussocky grass between the gravestones of the churchyard.

High above, a hawk sailed on the wind, its head turning slightly, this way and that, searching for prey.

Sir Guy was dressed in his finest; blue swallowtail coat, buff waistcoat, kerseymere breeches and hessian boots. He caused quite a stir in the church as everyone craned their necks to get a better view.

Annabelle only vaguely heard the words of the service.

178

'They that are after the flesh, do mind the things of the flesh; but they that are after the Spirit the things of the Spirit. For to be carnally minded is death.'

'Am I carnally minded?' thought Annabelle. 'I must be. I hate him, and I want him. Oh, Peter, where are you? And what have I done?

Sir Guy was yawning and fidgeting. 'This is curst dull,' he muttered to Annabelle behind the shelter of the Book of Common Prayer. 'This fellow does prose on so.'

'Shhh!' said Annabelle crossly, fearful that the sensitive Mr Pettifor would hear.

But even she had to admit that there was a soporific quality about Mr Pettifor's preaching. His voice droned against the window panes as a fly drones against the glass on a sunny day. Heads began to nod and from behind her rose an occasional snore.

And then the vestry door opened with a crash.

The vicar of St Charles and St Jude sprang to the pulpit, shoving his curate aside with his beefy shoulders. He grasped the brass eagle by both wings and glared down into the congregation. 'Where is he?' he demanded.

His eyes ranged over the upturned faces and then fastened on that of Sir Guy.

'Whoreson!' yelled the vicar, raising his whip. 'I'll have ye!'

To the congregation's amazement, he leapt agilely down from the pulpit and cracked his whip with a resounding snap.

Sir Guy rose like a rocketing pheasant and ran headlong down the aisle to the church door.

'*Hoic halloa!*' yelled the vicar. 'After him!'

He ran down the aisle, brandishing his whip. 'Papa!' screamed Annabelle.

'After him!' echoed the choir boys gleefully, scrambling over the choir stalls. 'After him!'

And soon most of the village of Hopeworth was in pursuit.

Out in the churchyard, Sir Guy twisted and turned and ran this way and that while the vicar's whip slashed across his shoulders.

He took the churchyard wall at a great leap and ran towards the village.

The vicar, followed by men, women and children, tumbled cheering after him. Bonnets and hats were flying, dresses were muddied and shoes ruined as the congregation of St Charles and St Jude cheerfully sacrificed their finery to the joys of the chase.

Sir Guy fled towards the inn. If only he could lock himself in his room until these demented yokels had cooled down.

He had nearly reached the inn door when he stood stock still and stared. Riding down on him was the figure of Squire Radford atop a huge roan horse, his little figure with old-fashioned wig and old-fashioned tricorne, breeches and gaiters crouched low over the reins.

'Swine!' shouted the little Squire bringing his whip down on Sir Guy's shoulders as he rode past at full gallop.

The whip twined itself around Sir Guy's neck and sent him spinning into the mud.

'Hold hard, Jimmy,' called the vicar as the great horse reared and plunged and finally came to a halt. 'Let hounds have 'im.'

'Hounds?' said the Squire breathlessly. 'My good man, have you brought out your pack?'

'Just them,' said the vicar cheerfully. The Squire twisted and looked down.

The vicar had stood back and the village boys had plunged on the wriggling figure of Sir Guy. To cheers from the men and screams from the women, they tore off his trousers, held them aloft like a trophy, and then threw him into the village pond.

'No,' screamed Annabelle running forwards. 'Stop them. Oh, stop them.'

The vicar put a comforting arm around his daughter's shoulders. 'Come along home, Bella,' he said. 'When you hear what I have to tell you, you'll wish for him to be hanged instead.'

Annabelle sat in her father's study and listened in horror as the story of Sir Guy's perfidy unfolded.

'And what makes it worse is that Brabington never even had a liaison with that Evans woman,' finished the vicar.

'I must go to him,' cried Annabelle, leaping up. 'What he must think of me!'

'Now then, calmly,' said the vicar. 'I have written to him explaining the whole. It is for him to come to you. No use you running to his country place and finding he's in London and running to London and finding he's on his way here. My stars, you could chase each other all over England by the end o' the week.'

'I have behaved most wickedly,' said Annabelle, sinking down in her chair again, 'and God has punished me.'

'Oh, you mustn't say that,' said the vicar. 'I mean, you've punished yourself, so it's no use blaming the Almighty.

'See, look at it this way. You didn't marry for love, you married to spite your sister. You start flirting about with a no-gooder like Sir Guy Wayne which, mark you, is a thing no virtuous female would ever consider, and so you reap the reward. All's well that ends well. Your husband will be here in under a couple of days, or my name is not Charles Armitage.'

'Am I such a bad person, papa?' asked Annabelle anxiously.

'Not you,' said the vicar. 'Not now. Time was when you had too much beauty and more hair than wit. But now I would say you'd definitely growed, Bella. Minerva spoiled you. She was always making excuses for your behaviour, you know. And me, I could never stand up to Minerva when she got that prissy look on her face.'

'Have you heard from her?' asked Annabelle.

'Not since they left Dover, but she'll be all right. She's in good hands.'

'Do you think he will really come?'

'Brabington? Of course. Now off with you. I'm so weak I can hardly lift my glass.'

For the next few days Annabelle could not bear to leave the vicarage. She sat by the parlour window, looking across the rain-washed fields, waiting to see his carriage turn the bend in the road.

But the Marquess of Brabington did not come. The post boy would blow a triumphant blast on his horn and she could hardly wait until he opened his bag. There were letters from the twins, a letter from Lady Godolphin, one from an old friend of her mother, but no letter from the Marquess.

The girls were excited over the prospect of attending an assembly at the nearby town of Hopeminster on Friday evening.

Daphne and Deirdre were to be allowed to dance for the first time, Frederica and Diana were to be allowed to go, provided they promised to sit quietly and watch the dancing.

Holden had added to the excitement by refurbishing their party dresses into the latest London fashions and promising to do their hair.

The housekeeper complained she could not get the kitchen to herself for a moment, the girls were so busy making washes and pomatums.

Annabelle had not thought for a moment that she would be free to go. But as Friday approached and still her husband did not arrive, she gave in to her sisters' urging and agreed to attend.

'You can't sit forever waiting for him, Bella,' said Deirdre sympathetically. 'Just think. He will probably ride into the ballroom on his charger, and sweep you away, like young Lochinvar.'

That made Annabelle smile, despite the strain that was beginning to show on her face. The vicar kept telling her cheerfully that she was a widgeon, a nodcock, he would come. But privately the vicar was beginning to entertain some doubts.

The Marquess's estates lay two counties away to the south. In order to reach London he had to pass through Hopeminster. He could have made the journey with one long day's hard riding. Now the vicar began to wonder if the man had taken his daughter in dislike and wanted no more to do with her despite that long letter of explanation.

It was up to Squire Radford to remind the vicar he had done all he could do and it was now in the hands of the Almighty.

But the vicar, after a long wrestle with his soul, decided this was not a very hopeful state of affairs. Had he not prayed and prayed for good hunting weather last winter, and had the Almighty not sent down one plaguey, frosty day after another?

It began to dawn on Annabelle's sisters that matters stood very badly with her. The humiliation of Sir Guy for some terrible wrong he had done Annabelle, the absence of her husband, and her refusal to talk about London worried them.

Deirdre was of a highly romantic and optimistic nature. She told the others that these things happened. That Bella should never have married in the first place, and no doubt she would console herself with some devilishly handsome man at the Assembly.

The little girls happily accepted Deirdre's explanation, and anytime Annabelle put forward a mild suggestion that she might forego the Assembly they shrieked with dismay and urged her to come. Someone would be waiting for her, they said mysteriously.

So insistent were they that Annabelle began to hope wildly her husband was going to be there, and that her family had planned it all as a secret surprise.

This hope was fuelled by a letter from the stern patronesses of Almack's which had been forwarded to Annabelle from London. In it, they explained stiffly that the refusal of her vouchers had been a mistake which had been brought to their notice by the Marquess of Brabington. They had much pleasure therefore in enclosing her vouchers. and so Annabelle began to hope and dream of seeing her husband soon. The letter from the patronesses had shown that, despite his fury with her, he *had* kept his promise and he had arranged for her to attend.

The vicar would soon have disabused her of such wild hopes, but Annabelle was in the state of mind where any hope was better than none, and so she did not ask him.

The day of the Assembly was a bustle of activity. Holden ironed and pinned and frizzed hair and tied ribbons, her thin wiry figure darting upstairs and downstairs.

At last they were all jammed in the travelling carriage and the vicar riding on the box to make room.

It was a clear moonlit night, to everyone's relief. A cloudy night would have meant their visit to the ball would have to be cancelled, for the roads were still muddy and treacherous after the recent rains.

Deirdre had pleaded in vain to be allowed to wear her hair up but had been greatly consoled by Holden who had brushed and wound her red hair into ringlets.

Annabelle was wearing a gown of silver gauze over a white slip. She wore a circlet of pearls on her blonde hair and a simple pearl necklace around her neck.

She could not help thinking that by rights she should have been making her come-out at Almack's that very week on her husband's arm.

London was lost to her. She often thought she would never see that city again, would never feel her husband's arm under hers as he led her up the stairs to some ballroom or rout.

Her physical craving for him was immense. Deirdre kept teasing her on the road to the ball about the dark and handsome man who would be waiting for her, and Annabelle sat engulfed in a suffocating wave of hope.

The Cock and Feathers was Hopeminster's main hostelry. Assemblies were held in a banqueting hall at the back and the society of Berham country came for miles around.

Mrs Armitage moaned feebly every time the carriage jolted over a rut in the road and protested she would be too ill to endure the rigours of the evening. But as the carriage swung into the coachyard of the inn and faint sounds of music could be heard, even Mrs Armitage forgot to be ill in the bustle of finding fans and reticules.

They were a trifle late so the company was mostly assembled. The vicar was relieved to see how beautiful, almost radiant, Annabelle looked as she was immediately surrounded by a court of admirers.

He did not know that Annabelle was sure her husband would walk through the door at any moment and she wanted him to see her looking at her best. But as country dance followed reel, and galop followed minuet – for the minuet was still danced in these rustic areas – Annabelle's spirits began to sink.

Pain throbbed behind her eyes. There seemed to be too much boisterous leaping and prancing. More than anything did she want to run away, to get home as fast as possible and bury her aching head under the pillows and have a good cry.

The Marquess of Brabington was tired and out of sorts. He had dealt firmly and well with the affairs of his estate. Now as he sat in the gloomy library of Brabington Court, he wondered what manner of man his predecessor had been.

He had met the late Marquess once many years ago and had only a hazy recollection of him. He must have been a curst dull stick, thought the Marquess, looking around the heavy gloomy furniture and rows and rows of dry books which had been bought from the bookseller by the yard and never opened.

Annabelle's pretty figure danced at the edge of his thoughts but he kept banishing it. He felt he was now the misogynist – or Missing Jest – that Lady Godolphin had once claimed him to be. He longed to return to the wars. He had been kept on in London, first because of his marriage, secondly as a reward for his bravery, and third, because Horse Guards had had intelligence of a Bonapartist spy who was abroad in London society and wished the Marquess to smoke him out. But although the

Marquess had questioned and listened and spent many weary hours drinking with suspects, he had not come across anyone who showed any signs of wishing to betray his country.

He was suddenly sick of his own company and resolved all at once to return to London.

He decided to ride rather than take his carriage. He would break his journey by staying with a friend on the far side of Hopeminster. And when he reached Hopeminster, he thought grimly, he would go on riding as hard as he could through the town in case unmanly weakness should drive him to take the road to Hopeworth.

He had searched the post every day, hoping for some letter from his wife. But nothing came. No one wrote at all. There had been some letter from Lady Godolphin but her servant had ridden hard through a deluge and when he had produced the letter it had been nothing more than a sopping bundle of parchment, the ink running in rivers and the writing quite obliterated. He assumed she had written to tell him of her forthcoming wedding.

He walked to the window and tugged aside the curtain. A small bright moon was riding high above the trees.

It was only eight o'clock. With luck he might reach his friend's on the other side of Hopeminster by eleven. He would pack a change of linen and his evening clothes in his saddle bags and leave as soon as he could.

In half an hour's time, he was riding down his drive and away from the great black bulk of Brabington Court. An ancient lodge keeper – all the servants were ancient – tottered out to swing open the gates.

The Marquess spurred his horse and rode off at full gallop.

But the hard exercise of riding would not banish his wife's face from his mind. Rather, it seemed to grow clearer as the miles flew back under his horse's thudding hooves.

By the time he reached the outskirts of Hopeminster and saw the white ribbon of the Hopeworth road branching off to his right, he found himself reining in his horse and

186

sitting very still under the bright light of the moon.

She was so near, he could sense her presence. He remembered the way she had looked at him as she lay against his chest and almost groaned aloud.

'She wants a separation,' he muttered. 'Be sensible.'

But it was with a great feeling of weariness and loss that he turned his horse's head in the direction of Hopeminster.

There seemed to be some sort of gala affair going on at the Cock and Feathers. There were sounds of music and laughing voices and the inn yard was full of carriages of every description.

He was sick of his own company and decided to stop for a drink at the tap.

He tossed a coin to an ostler and swung himself down from the saddle.

Mr Boyse, the landlord, was crossing the small hall of the inn when the Marquess made his entrance.

'Why, my lord,' he beamed, helping the Marquess out of his benjamin. 'We are mighty pleased to see you. And how goes Lord Sylvester? Well, you'll be looking for a room to change your clothes for the dance, and you're in luck, for one o' the gennlmun decoided he don't need it now, it bein' full moon. Said he would roid home later. Now if you'll ...'

'Stay,' said the Marquess. 'I have not come for any dance. I am simply stopping to have some refreshment before I proceed on my journey.'

The landlord looked puzzled, and then his face cleared. 'You'll be taking her ladyship with you, loik.'

'No,' said the Marquess. 'Her ladyship is at Hopeworth.'

'Don't you know, my lord? Her ladyship be *here*!'

'Here! Where?'

'Whoy at dance, to be sure, with vicar and all.'

The Marquess stood staring into space until the landlord began to wonder if his lordship's wits were wandering.

'Ah, yes,' said the Marquess at last. 'Get a fellow to

fetch my saddle bags. I will change directly.'

'Very good, my lord,' said Mr Boyse, looking at the Marquess curiously. 'Your room 'll be number noin.'

'I shall only need the use of the room for changing,' said the Marquess. 'I shall not be staying the night, nor shall I be staying long at the Assembly. Tell them to have my horse rubbed down, saddled and ready.'

The Marquess spent quite long over his toilet, arguing with his reflection in the dim looking glass. He owed it to himself, he thought savagely, to have one last word with her. He had sometimes dreamt that she was pining for him at the vicarage, realizing all she had so thoughtlessly, cruelly and carelessly thrown away.

But to find her at a ball! It was the outside of enough. He would give her a piece of his mind. Yes, and that conniving vicar as well.

When he entered the ballroom, the dance was in full progress. Hands across, down the middle flew the couples in a country dance.

And leading a set on the far side of the ballroom, partnered by a fresh-faced country gentleman, was his wife.

As he watched, she stumbled slightly and her partner laughed and caught her round the waist to steady her.

'Good heavens!' Annabelle's partner said, as he joined hands with her, 'Who is that handsome man glowering in the doorway like Satan himself?'

Annabelle's head snapped round. It was almost as if she knew who it would be in that split second before she turned her head.

She stopped stock still. 'Peter,' she whispered.

The other dancers stumbled into her and past her, looking at her curiously.

Annabelle completely forgot about her partner. She forgot about the dance. She walked slowly towards the Marquess as if there were no one else in the room.

She held out her hands to him, and, despite his anger, he found himself taking them and holding them in a tight clasp.

'You came after all, Peter,' said Annabelle, her eyes bright with tears. 'Deirdre hinted you would, but I had begun to lose hope.'

'I came only by chance,' he said coldly. 'I decided to give myself the luxury of telling you exactly what I think of you.'

Annabelle snatched her hands away. 'Then you do not love me,' she said. 'Despite the fact that father explained about Miss Evans and Sir Guy and the trick they played on me. You do not love me. And I,' her voice caught on a sob, 'I love you so much.'

'What?'

She made a move to turn away but he swung her around.

'What did you say?' he demanded.

'You do not know?' She looked at him. 'Did you not get father's letter?'

'Not that,' he said, his eyes searching her own. 'Did you say you loved me?'

Annabelle hung her head, all pride gone.

'Yes,' she said miserably.

The vicar bowled in from the card room a minute later to find the ballroom in dead silence. It seemed as if the whole of Berham county was standing in frozen silence watching the Marquess of Brabington ruthlessly kissing his wife.

'Here!' yelled the vicar. 'Is this a dance or a funeral? Come on, you fiddlers. Let's have a lively jig. Gentlemen, ladies, to your places!'

The company came to life, the music struck up, Deirdre, Daphne, Diana and Frederica Armitage all dried sentimental tears from their eyes.

'My children! cried Mrs Armitage, heading in Annabelle's direction, trailing wisps of chiffon and lace.

'Hey, leave 'em alone,' growled the vicar, catching hold of his wife. 'There's been enough Haymarket scenes for one evening.'

'Come away with me,' said the Marquess to Annabelle. 'Now! Let us spend the night together far away from this

189

brood of Armitages.'

'Oh, Peter,' cried Annabelle, 'only wait until I get my cloak!'

Soon they were jogging off through the night, an odd pair seated on one horse in all their ballroom finery.

Annabelle explained as they rode along about Sir Guy's plot, and his subsequent humiliation at the hands of the vicar.

'If he is still in town,' said the Marquess, 'I will call him out. But Annabelle, you do not know the worst of it. I am to leave for Portugal in a fortnight. I thought you were lost to me so I volunteered to rejoin my regiment.'

'You would have done that in any case,' said Annabelle, 'and I do not care, for I am going with you.'

'You cannot! You do not know the hardship, the death, the misery.'

'I do not want to be without you ever again,' said Annabelle.

'We will talk later,' he replied, holding her tightly as his horse stumbled.

'My poor Caesar is at the end of his tether,' he said. 'I have ridden him too hard this night. Look, yonder is an inn of sorts. We will need to put up there. I was going to stay with a friend, but I want you all to myself, so this inn will have to do.'

He reined in at an evil-looking inn which crouched under its heavy roof of ragged thatch beside the road.

'There's a light in the tap,' he said. He swung her down from the saddle.

A bleary-looking landlord came out to meet them, blinking at the sight of their glittering evening dress.

He had a room, he said apologetically, but he did not think it fit for the quality. If they would only ride on a few miles they would come to a regular posting house.

But the horse was too tired to go any further and the couple too happy to mind where they slept. The Marquess sent Annabelle up to the bedchamber while he attended to his horse and saw it stabled for the night.

Annabelle looked around the room with a shudder. The

plaster was old and cracked. The four-poster bed had dusty hangings and a whole family of worms seemed to have been sinking their teeth in the woodwork over the centuries.

But, she decided, when she went with her husband to the wars, she would need to become used to worse than this.

The Marquess came in, stooping his head under the low lintel of the door.

'This is awful,' he said, as he surveyed the neglected chamber. The blackened beams were so low that he could not straighten up. 'Let us find somewhere else.'

But she simply held out her arms to him and he caught her to him and promptly forgot about everything else.

Some time later, he freed his lips reluctantly and told her to make ready for bed as he was going to have a wash at the pump in the yard.

Annabelle happily undressed and climbed cautiously into bed, wearing only a thin petticoat. The sheets felt cold and damp and she wished he would hurry up.

At last he arrived back, wearing only his shirt and breeches which he proceeded to strip off. 'My sweeting,' said the Marquess, his voice muffled as he pulled the shirt over his head, 'I am going to make love to you until I can no more, for we have wasted so much time.'

'I wish you would hurry,' said Annabelle. ''Tis monstrous cold.'

He divested himself of the rest of his clothes, blew out the candle, and said with a laugh, 'Prepare my lady, for I am about to set you on fire.'

He ran lightly across the room and leapt on the bed, still laughing as he rolled over and caught her to him.

There was a great creaking and groaning and suddenly the bed quite simply collapsed, the mattress dropping through the frame onto the floor and sending the chamber pot rolling to the other side of the room.

They lay clutching each other as the four posts of the bed slowly caved in and the canopy fell down on top of them.

'Oh, Peter,' wailed Annabelle, 'we cannot possibly make love now. What are you doing? Stop it! No, don't. Do it again. Oh, *Peter!*'

The Assembly was nearing its end. Frederica had fallen asleep with her head on Diana's shoulder. Deirdre had danced every dance, her red ringlets flying.

Squire Radford settled himself down comfortably next to the vicar in the refreshment room, and indicated Deirdre with a nod of his head.

'That's the next Armitage to wed,' he said, 'or I'm not mistaken.'

'Hey!' The vicar, who had drunk overmuch and was feeling the effects, looked blearily at his daughter.

'Oh, no,' he said, ponderously, shaking his head. 'I'm worn to flinders with all this love business. Next one will be an arranged marriage. That way I'll have a bit o' peace and quiet. Think Brabington's happy now?'

'Oh, very happy,' said the Squire.

'In that case,' said the vicar thoughtfully, 'I hope my Bella told him how it was all thanks to me that they're together again. Hope she told him that, Jimmy!'

'And thanks to me,' put in the Squire.

'Hey? Ho! Yes, yes, yes, but you ain't the girl's father.'

'I don't see ...'

'Well, I hear Jefferson's selling some o' his hounds and a grateful Brabington just might sport the blunt.'

'May the Lord have mercy on your mercenary soul,' said the Squire piously.

'Amen to that,' said the vicar of St Charles and St Jude.

Chesney, Marinn
   The taming of Annabelle.